Clove

by

Susan Coolidge

The Echo Library 2007

Published by

The Echo Library

Echo Library
131 High St.
Teddington
Middlesex TW11 8HH

www.echo-library.com

Please report serious faults in the text to complaints@echo-library.com

ISBN 978-1-40684-850-2

CONTENTS

CHAPTER I.

A TALK ON THE DOORSTEPS.

It was one of those afternoons in late April which are as mild and balmy as any June day. The air was full of the chirps and twitters of nest-building birds, and of sweet indefinable odors from half-developed leaf-buds and cherry and pear blossoms. The wisterias overhead were thickly starred with pointed pearl-colored sacs, growing purpler with each hour, which would be flowers before long; the hedges were quickening into life, the long pensile willow-boughs and the honey-locusts hung in a mist of fine green against the sky, and delicious smells came with every puff of wind from the bed of white violets under the parlor windows.

Katy and Clover Carr, sitting with their sewing on the door-steps, drew in with every breath the sense of spring. Who does not know the delightfulness of that first sitting out of doors after a long winter's confinement? It seems like flinging the gauntlet down to the powers of cold. Hope and renovation are in the air. Life has conquered Death, and to the happy hearts in love with life there is joy in the victory. The two sisters talked busily as they sewed, but all the time an only half-conscious rapture informed their senses,—the sympathy of that which is immortal in human souls with the resurrection of natural things, which is the sure pledge of immortality.

It was nearly a year since Katy had come back from that too brief journey to Europe with Mrs. Ashe and Amy, about which some of you have read, and many things of interest to the Carr family had happened during the interval. The "Natchitoches" had duly arrived in New York in October, and presently afterward Burnet was convulsed by the appearance of a tall young fellow in naval uniform, and the announcement of Katy's engagement to Lieutenant Worthington.

It was a piece of news which interested everybody in the little town, for Dr. Carr was a universal friend and favorite. For a time he had been the only physician in the place; and though with the gradual growth of population two or three younger men had appeared to dispute the ground with him, they were forced for the most part to content themselves with doctoring the new arrivals, and with such fragments and leavings of practice as Dr. Carr chose to intrust to them. None of the old established families would consent to call in any one else if they could possibly get the "old" doctor.

A skilful practitioner, who is at the same time a wise adviser, a helpful friend, and an agreeable man, must necessarily command a wide influence. Dr. Carr was "by all odds and far away," as our English cousins would express it, the most popular person in Burnet, wanted for all pleasant occasions, and doubly wanted for all painful ones.

So the news of Katy's engagement was made a matter of personal concern by a great many people, and caused a general stir, partly because she was her father's daughter, and partly because she was herself; for Katy had won many friends by her own merit. So long as Ned Worthington stayed, a sort of tide of congratulation and sympathy seemed to sweep through the house all day long. Tea-roses and chrysanthemums, and baskets of pears and the beautiful Burnet grapes flooded the premises, and the door-bell rang so often that Clover threatened to leave the door open, with a card attached,—"Walk straight in. *He* is in the parlor!"

Everybody wanted to see and know Katy's lover, and to have him as a guest. Ten tea-drinkings a week would scarcely have contented Katy's well-wishers, had the limitations of mortal weeks permitted such a thing; and not a can of oysters would have been left in the place if Lieutenant Worthington's leave had lasted three days longer. Clover and Elsie loudly complained that they themselves never had a chance to see him; for whenever he was not driving or walking with Katy, or having long *tête-à-têtes* in the library, he was eating muffins somewhere, or making calls on old ladies whose feelings would be dreadfully hurt if he went away without their seeing him.

"Sisters seem to come off worst of all," protested Johnnie. But in spite of their lamentations they all saw enough of their future brother-in-law to grow fond of him; and notwithstanding some natural pangs of jealousy at having to share Katy with an outsider, it was a happy visit, and every one was sorry when the leave of absence ended, and Ned had to go away.

A month later the "Natchitoches" sailed for the Bahamas. It was to be a six months' cruise only; and on her return she was for a while to make part of the home squadron. This furnished a good opportunity for her first lieutenant to marry; so it was agreed that the wedding should take place in June, and Katy set about her preparations in the leisurely and simple fashion which was characteristic of her. She had no ambition for a great *trousseau*, and desired to save her father expense; so her outfit, as compared with that of most modern brides, was a very moderate one, but being planned and mostly made at home, it necessarily involved thought, time, and a good deal of personal exertion.

Dear little Clover flung herself into the affair with even more interest than if it had been her own. Many happy mornings that winter did the sisters spend together over their dainty stitches and "white seam." Elsie and Johnnie were good needle-women now, and could help in many ways. Mrs. Ashe often joined them; even Amy could contribute aid in the plainer sewing, and thread everybody's needles. But the most daring and indefatigable of all was Clover, who never swerved in her determination that Katy's "things" should be as nice and as pretty as love and industry combined could make them. Her ideas as to decoration soared far beyond Katy's. She hem-stitched, she cat-stitched, she feather-stitched, she lace-stitched, she tucked and frilled and embroidered, and generally worked her fingers off; while the bride vainly protested that all this finery was quite unnecessary, and that simple hems and a little Hamburg edging would answer just as well. Clover merely repeated the words, "Hamburg edging!" with an accent of scorn, and went straight on in her elected way.

As each article received its last touch, and came from the laundry white and immaculate, it was folded to perfection, tied with a narrow blue or pale rose-colored ribbon, and laid aside in a sacred receptacle known as "The Wedding Bureau." The handkerchiefs, grouped in dozens, were strewn with dried violets and rose-leaves to make them sweet. Lavender-bags and sachets of orris lay among the linen; and perfumes as of Araby were discernible whenever a drawer in the bureau was pulled out.

So the winter passed, and now spring was come; and the two girls on the doorsteps were talking about the wedding, which seemed very near now.

"Tell me just what sort of an affair you want it to be," said Clover.

"It seems more your wedding than mine, you have worked so hard for it," replied Katy. "You might give your ideas first."

"My ideas are not very distinct. It's only lately that I have begun to think about it at all, there has been so much to do. I'd like to have you have a beautiful dress and a great many wedding-presents and everything as pretty as can be, but not so many bridesmaids as Cecy, because there is always such a fuss in getting them nicely up the aisle in church and out again,—that is as far as I've got. But so long as you are pleased, and it goes off well, I don't care exactly how it is managed."

"Then, since you are in such an accommodating frame of mind, it seems a good time to break my views to you. Don't be shocked, Clovy; but, do you know, I don't want to be married in church at all, or to have any bridesmaids, or anything arranged for beforehand particularly. I should like things to be simple, and to just *happen*."

"But, Katy, you can't do it like that. It will all get into a snarl if there is no planning beforehand or rehearsals; it would be confused and horrid."

"I don't see why it would be confused if there were nothing to confuse. Please not be vexed; but I always have hated the ordinary kind of wedding, with its fuss and worry and so much of everything, and just like all the other weddings, and the bride looking tired to death, and nobody enjoying it a bit. I'd like mine to be different, and more—more—real. I don't want any show or processing about, but just to have things nice and pretty, and all the people I love and who love me to come to it, and nothing cut and dried, and nobody tired, and to make it a sort of dear, loving occasion, with leisure to realize how dear it is and what it all means. Don't you think it would really be nicer in that way?"

"Well, yes, as you put it, and 'viewed from the higher standard,' as Miss Inches would say, perhaps it would. Still, bridesmaids and all that are very pretty to look at; and folks will be surprised if you don't have them."

"Never mind folks," remarked the irreverent Katy. "I don't care a button for that argument. Yes; bridesmaids and going up the aisle in a long procession and all the rest *are* pretty to look at,—or were before they got to be so hackneyed. I can imagine the first bridal procession up the aisle of some early cathedral as having been perfectly beautiful. But nowadays, when the butcher and baker and candlestick-maker and everybody else do it just alike, the custom seems to me to have lost its charm. I never did enjoy having things exactly as every one else has them,—all going in the same direction like a flock of sheep. I would like my little wedding to be something especially my own. There was a poetical meaning in those old customs; but now that the custom has swallowed up so much of the meaning, it would please me better to retain the meaning and drop the custom."

"I see what you mean," said Clover, not quite convinced, but inclined as usual to admire Katy and think that whatever she meant must be right. "But tell me a little more. You mean to have a wedding-dress, don't you?" doubtfully.

"Yes, indeed!"

"Have you thought what it shall be?"

"Do you recollect that beautiful white crape shawl of mamma's which papa gave me two years ago? It has a lovely wreath of embroidery round it; and it came to me the other day that it would make a charming gown, with white surah or something for the under-dress. I should like that better than anything new, because mamma used to wear it, and it would seem as if she were here still, helping me to get ready. Don't you think so?"

"It is a lovely idea," said Clover, the ever-ready tears dimming her happy blue eyes for a moment, "and just like you. Yes, that shall be the dress,—dear mamma's shawl. It will please papa too, I think, to have you choose it."

"I thought perhaps it would," said Katy, soberly. "Then I have a wide white watered sash which Aunt Izzy gave me, and I mean to have that worked into the dress somehow. I should like to wear something of hers too, for she was really good to us when we were little, and all that long time that I was ill; and we were not always good to her, I am afraid. Poor Aunt Izzy! What troublesome little wretches we were,—I most of all!"

"Were you? Somehow I never can recollect the time when you were not a born angel. I am afraid I don't remember Aunt Izzy well. I just have a vague memory of somebody who was pretty strict and cross."

"Ah, you never had a back, and needed to be waited on night and day, or you would recollect a great deal more than that. Cousin Helen helped me to appreciate what Aunt Izzy really was. By the way, one of the two things I have set my heart on is to have Cousin Helen come to my wedding."

"It would be lovely if she could. Do you suppose there is any chance?"

"I wrote her week before last, but she hasn't answered yet. Of course it depends on how she is; but the accounts from her have been pretty good this year."

"What is the other thing you have set your heart on? You said 'two.'"

"The other is that Rose Red shall be here, and little Rose. I wrote to her the other day also, and coaxed hard. Wouldn't it be too enchanting? You know how we have always longed to have her in Burnet; and if she could come now it would make everything twice as pleasant."

"Katy, what an enchanting thought!" cried Clover, who had not seen Rose since they all left Hillsover. "It would be the greatest lark that ever was to have the Roses. When do you suppose we shall hear? I can hardly wait, I am in such a hurry to have her say 'Yes.'"

"But suppose she says 'No'?"

"I won't think of such a possibility. Now go on. I suppose your principles don't preclude a wedding-cake?"

"On the contrary, they include a great deal of wedding-cake. I want to send a box to everybody in Burnet,—all the poor people, I mean, and the old people and the children at the Home and those forlorn creatures at the poor-house and all papa's patients."

"But, Katy, that will cost a lot," objected the thrifty Clover.

"I know it; so we must do it in the cheapest way, and make the cake ourselves. I have Aunt Izzy's recipe, which is a very good one; and if we all take hold, it won't be such an immense piece of work. Debby has quantities of raisins stoned already. She has been doing them in the evenings a few at a time for the last month. Mrs. Ashe knows a factory where you can get the little white boxes for ten dollars a thousand, and I have commissioned her to send for five hundred."

"Five hundred! What an immense quantity!"

"Yes; but there are all the Hillsover girls to be remembered, and all our kith and kin, and everybody at the wedding will want one. I don't think it will be too many. Oh, I have arranged it all in my mind. Johnnie will slice the citron, Elsie will wash the currants, Debby measure and bake, Alexander mix, you and I will attend to the icing, and all of us will cut it up."

"Alexander!"

"Alexander. He is quite pleased with the idea, and has constructed an implement—a sort of spade, cut out of new pine wood—for the purpose. He says it will be a sight easier than digging flower-beds. We will set about it next week; for the cake improves by keeping, and as it is the heaviest job we have to do, it will be well to get it out of the way early."

"Sha'n't you have a floral bell, or a bower to stand in, or something of that kind?" ventured Clover, timidly.

"Indeed I shall not," replied Katy. "I particularly dislike floral bells and bowers. They are next worst to anchors and harps and 'floral pillows' and all the rest of the dreadful things that they have at funerals. No, we will have plenty of fresh flowers, but not in stiff arrangements. I want it all to seem easy and to *be* easy. Don't look so disgusted, Clovy."

"Oh, I'm not disgusted. It's your wedding. I want you to have everything in your own way."

"It's everybody's wedding, I think," said Katy, tenderly. "Everybody is so kind about it. Did you see the thing that Polly sent this morning?"

"No. It must have come after I went out. What was it?"

"Seven yards of beautiful nun's lace which she bought in Florence. She says it is to trim a morning dress; but it's really too pretty. How dear Polly is! She sends me something almost every day. I seem to be in her thoughts all the time. It is because she loves Ned so much, of course; but it is just as kind of her."

"I think she loves you almost as much as Ned," said Clover.

"Oh, she couldn't do that; Ned is her only brother. There is Amy at the gate now."

It was a much taller Amy than had come home from Italy the year before who was walking toward them under the budding locust-boughs. Roman fever had seemed to quicken and stimulate all Amy's powers, and she had grown very fast during the past year. Her face was as frank and childlike as ever, and her eyes as blue; but she was prettier than when she went to Europe, for her cheeks were pink, and the mane of waving hair which framed them in was very becoming. The hair was just long enough now to touch her shoulders; it was turning brown as it lengthened, but the ends of the locks still shone with childish gold, and caught the sun in little shining rings as it filtered down through the tree branches.

She kissed Clover several times, and gave Katy a long, close hug; then she produced a parcel daintily hid in silver paper.

"Tanta," she said,—this was a pet name lately invented for Katy,—"here is something for you from mamma. It's something quite particular, I think, for mamma cried when she was writing the note; not a hard cry, you know, but just two little teeny-weeny tears in her eyes. She kept smiling, though, and she looked happy, so I guess it isn't anything very bad. She said I was to give it to you with her best, *best* love."

Katy opened the parcel, and beheld a square veil of beautiful old blonde. The note said:

This was my wedding-veil, dearest Katy, and my mother wore it
before me. It has been laid aside all these years with the idea
that perhaps Amy might want it some day; but instead I send it
to you, without whom there would be no Amy to wear this or
anything else. I think it would please Ned to see it on your
head, and I know it would make me very happy; but if you don't
feel like using it, don't mind for a moment saying so to

Your loving
POLLY.

Katy handed the note silently to Clover, and laid her face for a little while among the soft folds of the lace, about which a faint odor of roses hung like the breath of old-time and unforgotten loves and affections.

"Shall you?" queried Clover, softly.

"Why, of course! Doesn't it seem too sweet? Both our mothers!"

"There!" cried Amy, "you are going to cry too, Tanta! I thought weddings were nice funny things. I never supposed they made people feel badly. I sha'n't ever let Mabel get married, I think. But she'll have to stay a little girl always in that case, for I certainly won't have her an old maid."

"What do you know about old maids, midget?" asked Clover.

"Why, Miss Clover, I have seen lots of them. There was that one at the Pension Suisse; you remember, Tanta? And the two on the steamer when we came home. And there's Miss Fitz who made my blue frock; Ellen said she was a regular old maid. I never mean to let Mabel be like that."

"I don't think there's the least danger," remarked Katy, glancing at the inseparable Mabel, who was perched on Amy's arm, and who did not look a day older than she had done eighteen months previously. "Amy, we're going to make wedding-cake next week,—heaps and heaps of wedding-cake. Don't you want to come and help?"

"Why, of course I do. What fun! Which day may I come?"

The cake-making did really turn out fun. Many hands made light work of what would have been a formidable job for one or two. It was all done gradually. Johnnie cut the golden citron quarters into thin transparent slices in the sitting-room one morning while the others were sewing, and reading Tennyson aloud. Elsie and Amy made a regular frolic of the currant-washing. Katy, with Debby's assistance, weighed and measured; and the mixture was enthusiastically stirred by Alexander, with the "spade" which he had invented, in a large new wash-tub. Then came the baking, which for two days filled the house with spicy, plum-puddingy odors; then the great feat of icing the big square loaves; and then the cutting up, in which all took part. There was much careful measurement that the slices might be an exact fit; and the kitchen rang with bright laughter and chat as Katy and Clover wielded the sharp bread-knives, and the others fitted the portions into their boxes, and tied the ribbons in crisp little bows. Many delicious crumbs and odd corners and fragments fell to the share of the younger workers; and altogether the occasion struck Amy as so enjoyable that she announced—with her mouth full—that she had changed her mind, and that Mabel might get married as often as she pleased, if she would have cake like *that* every time,—a liberality of permission which Mabel listened to with her invariable waxen smile.

When all was over, and the last ribbons tied, the hundreds of little boxes were stacked in careful piles on a shelf of the inner closet of the doctor's office to wait till they were wanted,—an arrangement which naughty Clover pronounced eminently suitable, since there should always be a doctor close at hand where there was so much wedding-cake. But before all this was accomplished, came what Katy, in imitation of one of Miss Edgeworth's heroines, called "The Day of Happy Letters."

CHAPTER II.

THE DAY OF HAPPY LETTERS.

The arrival of the morning boat with letters and newspapers from the East was the great event of the day in Burnet. It was due at eleven o'clock; and everybody, consciously or unconsciously, was on the lookout for it. The gentlemen were at the office bright and early, and stood chatting with each other, and fingering the keys of their little drawers till the rattle of the shutter announced that the mail was distributed. Their wives and daughters at home, meanwhile, were equally in a state of expectation, and whatever they might be doing kept ears and eyes on the alert for the step on the gravel and the click of the latch which betokened the arrival of the family news-bringer.

Doctors cannot command their time like other people, and Dr. Carr was often detained by his patients, and made late for the mail, so it was all the pleasanter a surprise when on the great day of the cake-baking he came in earlier than usual, with his hands quite full of letters and parcels. All the girls made a rush for him at once; but he fended them off with an elbow, while with teasing slowness he read the addresses on the envelopes.

"Miss Carr—Miss Carr—Miss Katherine Carr—Miss Carr again; four for you, Katy. Dr. P. Carr,—a bill and a newspaper, I perceive; all that an old country doctor with a daughter about to be married ought to expect, I suppose. Miss Clover E. Carr,—one for the 'Confidante in white linen.' Here, take it, Clovy. Miss Carr again. Katy, you have the lion's share. Miss Joanna Carr,—in the unmistakable handwriting of Miss Inches. Miss Katherine Carr, care Dr. Carr. That looks like a wedding present, Katy. Miss Elsie Carr; Cecy's hand, I should say. Miss Carr once more,—from the conquering hero, judging from the post-mark. Dr. Carr,—another newspaper, and—hollo!—one more for Miss Carr. Well, children, I hope for once you are satisfied with the amount of your correspondence. My arm fairly aches with the weight of it. I hope the letters are not so heavy inside as out."

"I am quite satisfied, Papa, thank you," said Katy, looking up with a happy smile from Ned's letter, which she had torn open first of all. "Are you going, dear?" She laid her packages down to help him on with his coat. Katy never forgot her father.

"Yes, I am going. Time and rheumatism wait for no man. You can tell me your news when I come back."

It is not fair to peep into love letters, so I will only say of Ned's that it was very long, very entertaining,—Katy thought,—and contained the pleasant information that the "Natchitoches" was to sail four days after it was posted, and would reach New York a week sooner than any one had dared to hope. The letter contained several other things as well, which showed Katy how continually she had been in his thoughts,—a painting on rice paper, a dried flower or two, a couple of little pen-and-ink sketches of the harbor of Santa Lucia and the shipping, and a small cravat of an odd convent lace folded very flat and smooth.

Altogether it was a delightful letter, and Katy read it, as it were, in leaps, her eyes catching at the salient points, and leaving the details to be dwelt upon when she should be alone.

This done, she thrust the letter into her pocket, and proceeded to examine the others. The first was in Cousin Helen's clear, beautiful handwriting:—

DEAR KATY,—If any one had told us ten years ago that in this particular year of grace you would be getting ready to be married, and I preparing to come to your wedding, I think we should have listened with some incredulity, as to an agreeable fairy tale which could not possibly come true. We didn't look much like it, did we,—you in your big chair and I on my sofa? Yet here we are! When your letter first reached me it seemed a sort of impossible thing that I should accept your invitation; but the more I thought about it the more I felt as if I must, and now things seem to be working round to that end quite marvellously. I have had a good winter, but the doctor wishes me to try the experiment of the water cure again which benefited me so much the summer of your accident. This brings me in your direction; and I don't see why I might not come a little earlier than I otherwise should, and have the great pleasure of seeing you married, and making acquaintance with Lieutenant Worthington. That is, if you are perfectly sure that to have at so busy a time a guest who, like the Queen of Spain, has the disadvantage of being without legs, will not be more care than enjoyment. Think seriously over this point, and don't send for me unless you are certain. Meanwhile, I am making ready. Alex and Emma and little Helen—who is a pretty big Helen now—are to be my escorts as far as Buffalo on their way to Niagara. After that is all plain sailing, and Jane Carter and I can manage very well for ourselves. It seems like a dream to think that I may see you all so soon; but it is such a pleasant one that I would not wake up on any account.

I have a little gift which I shall bring you myself, my Katy; but I have a fancy also that you shall wear some trifling thing on your wedding-day which comes from me, so for fear of being forestalled I will say now, please don't buy any stockings for the occasion, but wear the pair which go with this, for the sake of your loving

COUSIN HELEN.

"These must be they," cried Elsie, pouncing on one of the little packages. "May I cut the string, Katy?"

Permission was granted; and Elsie cut the string. It was indeed a pair of beautiful white silk stockings embroidered in an open pattern, and far finer than anything which Katy would have thought of choosing for herself.

"Don't they look exactly like Cousin Helen?" she said, fondling them. "Her things always are choicer and prettier than anybody's else, somehow. I can't think how she does it, when she never by any chance goes into a shop. Who can this be from, I wonder?"

"This" was the second little package. It proved to contain a small volume bound in white and gold, entitled, "Advice to Brides." On the fly-leaf appeared this inscription:—

To Katherine Carr, on the occasion of her approaching bridal, from her affectionate teacher,

MARIANNE NIPSON.

1 Timothy, ii. 11.

Clover at once ran to fetch her Testament that she might verify the quotation, and announced with a shriek of laughter that it was: "Let the women learn in silence with all subjection;" while Katy, much diverted, read extracts casually selected from the work, such as: "A wife should receive her husband's decree without cavil or question, remembering that the husband is the head of the wife, and that in all matters of dispute his opinion naturally and scripturally outweighs her own."

Or: "'A soft answer turneth away wrath.' If your husband comes home fretted and impatient, do not answer him sharply, but soothe him with gentle words and caresses. Strict attention to the minor details of domestic management will often avail to secure peace."

And again: "Keep in mind the epitaph raised in honor of an exemplary wife of the last century,—'She never banged the door.' Qualify yourself for a similar testimonial."

"Tanta never does bang doors," remarked Amy, who had come in as this last "elegant extract" was being read.

"No, that's true; she doesn't," said Clover. "Her prevailing vice is to leave them open. I like that truth about a good dinner 'availing' to secure peace, and the advice to 'caress' your bear when he is at his crossest. Ned never does issue 'decrees,' though, I fancy; and on the whole, Katy, I don't believe Mrs. Nipson's present is going to be any particular comfort in your future trials. Do read something else to take the taste out of our mouths. We will listen in 'all subjection.'"

Katy was already deep in a long epistle from Rose.

"This is too delicious," she said; "do listen." And she began again at the beginning:—

MY SWEETEST OF ALL OLD SWEETS,—Come to your wedding! Of course

I shall. It would never seem to me to have any legal sanction whatever if I were not there to add my blessing. Only let me

know which day "early in June" it is to be, that I may make
ready. Deniston will fetch us on, and by a special piece of good
luck, a man in Chicago—whose name I shall always bless if only
I can remember what it is—has been instigated by our mutual
good angel to want him on business just about that time; so that
he would have to go West anyway, and would rather have me along
than not, and is perfectly resigned to his fate. I mean to come
three days before, and stay three days after the wedding, if I
may, and altogether it is going to be a lark of larks. Little
Rose can talk quite fluently now, and almost read; that is, she
knows six letters of her picture alphabet. She composes poems
also. The other day she suddenly announced,—

"Mamma, I have made up a sort of a im. May I say it to you?"

I naturally consented, and this was the

IM.

> Jump in the parlor,
> Jump in the hall,
> God made us all!

Now did you ever hear of anything quite so dear as that, for a
baby only three years and five months old? I tell you she is a
wonder. You will all adore her, Clover particularly. Oh, my dear
little C.! To think I am going to see her!

I met both Ellen Gray and Esther Dearborn the other day, and
where do you think it was? At Mary Silver's wedding! Yes, she is
actually married to the Rev. Charles Playfair Strothers, and
settled in a little parsonage somewhere in the Hoosac
Tunnel,—or near it,—and already immersed in "duties." I can't
think what arguments he used to screw her up to the rash act;
but there she is.

It wasn't exactly what one would call a cheerful wedding. All
the connection took it very seriously; and Mary's uncle, who
married her, preached quite a lengthy funeral discourse to the
young couple, and got them nicely ready for death, burial, and
the next world, before he would consent to unite them for this.
He was a solemn-looking old person, who had been a missionary,
and "had laid away three dear wives in foreign lands," as he
confided to me afterward over a plate of ice-cream. He seemed
to me to be "taking notice," as they say of babies, and it is

barely possible that he mistook me for a single woman, for his attentions were rather pronounced till I introduced my husband prominently into conversation; after that he seemed more attracted by Ellen Gray.

Mary cried straight through the ceremony. In fact, I imagine she cried straight through the engagement, for her eyes looked wept out and had scarlet rims, and she was as white as her veil. In fact, whiter, for that was made of beautiful *point de Venise*, and was just a trifle yellowish. Everybody cried. Her mother and sister sobbed aloud, so did several maiden aunts and a grandmother or two and a few cousins. The church resounded with guggles and gasps, like a great deal of bath-water running out of an ill-constructed tub. Mr. Silver also wept, as a business man may, in a series of sniffs interspersed with silk handkerchief; you know the kind. Altogether it was a most cheerless affair. I seemed to be the only person present who was not in tears; but I really didn't see anything to cry about, so far as I was concerned, though I felt very hard-hearted.

I had to go alone, for Deniston was in New York. I got to the church rather early, and my new spring bonnet—which is a superior one—seemed to impress the ushers, so they put me in a very distinguished front pew all by myself. I bore my honors meekly, and found them quite agreeable, in fact,—you know I always did like to be made much of,—so you can imagine my disgust when presently three of the stoutest ladies you ever saw came sailing up the aisle, and prepared to invade *my* pew.

"Please move up, Madam," said the fattest of all, who wore a wonderful yellow hat.

But I was not "raised" at Hillsover for nothing, and remembering the success of our little ruse on the railroad train long ago, I stepped out into the aisle, and with my sweetest smile made room for them to pass.

"Perhaps I would better keep the seat next the door," I murmured to the yellow lady, "in case an attack should come on."

"An attack!" she repeated in an accent of alarm. She whispered to the others. All three eyed me suspiciously, while I stood looking as pensive and suffering as I could. Then after confabulating together for a little, they all swept into the seat behind mine, and I heard them speculating in low tones as to whether it was epilepsy or catalepsy or convulsions that I was subject to. I presume they made signs to all the other people who came in to steer clear of the lady with fits, for nobody invaded my privacy, and I sat in lonely splendor with a pew to myself, and was very comfortable indeed.

Mary's dress was white satin, with a great deal of point lace and pearl passementerie, and she wore a pair of diamond ear-rings which her father gave her, and a bouquet almost but not quite as large, which was the gift of the bridegroom. He has a nice face, and I think Silvery Mary will be happy with him, much happier than with her rather dismal family, though his salary is only fifteen hundred a year, and pearl passementerie, I believe, quite unknown and useless in the Hoosac region. She had loads of the most beautiful presents you ever saw. All the Silvers are rolling in riches, you know. One little thing made me laugh, for it was so like her. When the clergyman said, "Mary, wilt thou take this man to be thy wedded husband?" I distinctly saw her put her fingers over her mouth in the old, frightened way. It was only for a second, and after that I rather think Mr. Strothers held her hand tight for fear she might do it again. She sent her love to you, Katy. What sort of a gown are *you* going to have, by the way?

I have kept my best news to the last, which is that Deniston has at last given way, and we are to move into town in October. We have taken a little house in West Cedar Street. It is quite small and very dingy and I presume inconvenient, but I already love it to distraction, and feel as if I should sit up all night for the first month to enjoy the sensation of being no longer that horrid thing, a resident of the suburbs. I hunt the paper shops and collect samples of odd and occult pattern, and compare them with carpets, and am altogether in my element, only longing for the time to come when I may put together my pots and pans and betake me across the mill-dam. Meantime, Roslein is living in a state of quarantine. She is not permitted to speak with any other children, or even to look out of window at one, for fear she may contract some sort of contagious disease, and spoil our beautiful visit to Burnet. She sends you a kiss, and so do I; and mother and Sylvia and Deniston and grandmamma, particularly, desire their love.

Your loving

ROSE RED.

"Oh," cried Clover, catching Katy round the waist, and waltzing wildly about the room, "what a delicious letter! What fun we are going to have! It seems too good to be true. Tum-ti-ti, tum-ti-ti. Keep step, Katy. I forgive you for the first time for getting married. I never did before, really and truly. Tum-ti-ti; I am so happy that I must dance!"

"There go my letters," said Katy, as with the last rapid twirl, Rose's many-sheeted epistle and the "Advice to Brides" flew to right and left. "There go two of your hair-pins, Clover. Oh, do stop; we shall all be in pieces."

Clover brought her gyrations to a close by landing her unwilling partner suddenly on the sofa. Then with a last squeeze and a rapid kiss she began to pick up the scattered letters.

"Now read the rest," she commanded, "though anything else will sound flat after Rose's."

"Hear this first," said Elsie, who had taken advantage of the pause to open her own letter. "It is from Cecy, and she says she is coming to spend a month with her mother on purpose to be here for Katy's wedding. She sends heaps of love to you, Katy, and says she only hopes that Mr. Worthington will prove as perfectly satisfactory in all respects as her own dear Sylvester."

"My gracious, I should hope he would," put in Clover, who was still in the wildest spirits. "What a dear old goose Cecy is! I never hankered in the least for Sylvester Slack, did you, Katy?"

"Certainly not. It would be a most improper proceeding if I had," replied Katy, with a laugh. "Whom do you think this letter is from, girls? Do listen to it. It's written by that nice old Mr. Allen Beach, whom we met in London. Don't you recollect my telling you about him?"

MY DEAR MISS CARR,—Our friends in Harley Street have told me a piece of news concerning you which came to them lately in a letter from Mrs. Ashe, and I hope you will permit me to offer you my most sincere congratulations and good wishes. I recollect meeting Lieutenant Worthington when he was here two years ago, and liking him very much. One is always glad in a foreign land to be able to show so good a specimen of one's young countrymen as he affords,—not that England need be counted as a foreign country by any American, and least of all by myself, who have found it a true home for so many years.

As a little souvenir of our week of sight-seeing together, of which I retain most agreeable remembrances, I have sent you by my friends the Sawyers, who sail for America shortly, a copy of Hare's "Walks in London," which a young *protégée* of mine has for the past year been illustrating with photographs of the many curious old buildings described. You took so much interest in them while here that I hope you may like to see them again. Will you please accept with it my most cordial wishes for your future, and believe me

Very faithfully your friend,
ALLEN BEACH.

"What a nice letter!" said Clover.

"Isn't it?" replied Katy, with shining eyes, "what a thing it is to be a gentleman, and to know how to say and do things in the right way! I am so surprised and pleased that Mr. Beach should remember me. I never supposed he would, he sees so many people in London all the time, and it is quite a long time since we were there, nearly two years. Was your letter from Miss Inches, John?"

"Yes, and Mamma Marian sends you her love; and there's a present coming by express for you,—some sort of a book with a hard name. I can scarcely make it out, the Ru—ru—something of Omar Kay—y—Well, anyway it's a book, and she hopes you will read Emerson's 'Essay on Friendship' over before you are married, because it's a helpful utterance, and adjusts the mind to mutual conditions."

"Worse than 1 Timothy, ii. 11," muttered Clover. "Well, Katy dear, what next? What *are* you laughing at?"

"You will never guess, I am sure. This is a letter from Miss Jane! And she has made me this pincushion!"

The pincushion was of a familiar type, two circles of pasteboard covered with gray silk, neatly over-handed together, and stuck with a row of closely fitting pins. Miss Jane's note ran as follows:—

HILLSOVER, April 21.

DEAR KATY,—I hear from Mrs. Nipson that you are to be married shortly, and I want to say that you have my best wishes for your future. I think a man ought to be happy who has you for a wife. I only hope the one you have chosen is worthy of you. Probably he isn't, but perhaps you won't find it out. Life is a knotty problem for most of us. May you solve it satisfactorily to yourself and others! I have nothing to send but my good wishes and a few pins. They are not an unlucky present, I believe, as scissors are said to be.

Remember me to your sister, and believe me to be with true regard,
Yours, JANE A. BANGS.

"Dear me, is that her name?" cried Clover. "I always supposed she was baptized 'Miss Jane.' It never occurred to me that she had any other title. What appropriate initials! How she used to J.A.B. with us!"

"Now, Clovy, that's not kind. It's a very nice note indeed, and I am touched by it. It's a beautiful compliment to say that the man ought to be happy who has got me, I think. I never supposed that Miss Jane could pay a compliment."

"Or make a joke! That touch about the scissors is really jocose,—for Miss Jane. Rose Red will shriek over the letter and that particularly rigid pincushion.

They are both of them so exactly like her. Dear me! only one letter left. Who is that from, Katy? How fast one does eat up one's pleasures!"

"But you had a letter yourself. Surely papa said so. What was that? You haven't read it to us."

"No, for it contains a secret which you are not to hear just yet," replied Clover. "Brides mustn't ask questions. Go on with yours."

"Mine is from Louisa Agnew,—quite a long one, too. It's an age since we heard from her, you know."

ASHBURN, April 24.

DEAR KATY,—Your delightful letter and invitation came day before yesterday, and thank you for both. There is nothing in the world that would please me better than to come to your wedding if it were possible, but it simply isn't. If you lived in New Haven now, or even Boston,—but Burnet is so dreadfully far off, it seems as inaccessible as Kamchatka to a person who, like myself, has a house to keep and two babies to take care of.

Don't look so alarmed. The house is the same house you saw when you were here, and so is one of the babies; the other is a new acquisition just two years old, and as great a darling as Daisy was at the same age. My mother has been really better in health since he came, but just now she is at a sort of Rest Cure in Kentucky; and I have my hands full with papa and the children, as you can imagine, so I can't go off two days' journey to a wedding,—not even to yours, my dearest old Katy. I shall think about you all day long on *the* day, when I know which it is, and try to imagine just how everything looks; and yet I don't find that quite easy, for somehow I fancy that your wedding will be a little different from the common run. You always were different from other people to me, you know,—you and Clover,—and I love you so much, and I always shall.

Papa has taken a kit-kat portrait of me in oils,—and a blue dress,—which he thinks is like, and which I am going to send you as soon as it comes home from the framers. I hope you will like it a little for my sake. Dear Katy, I send so much love with it.

I have only seen the Pages in the street since they came home from Europe; but the last piece of news here is Lilly's engagement to Comte Ernest de Conflans. He has something to do with the French legation in Washington, I believe; and they crossed in the same steamer. I saw him driving with her the other day,—a little man, not handsome, and very dark. I do not know when they are to be married. Your Cousin Clarence is in Colorado.

    With two kisses apiece and a great hug for you, Katy, I am always
Your affectionate friend,
LOUISA.

    "Dear me!" said the insatiable Clover, "is that the very last? I wish we had another mail, and twelve more letters coming in at once. What a blessed institution the post-office is!"

CHAPTER III.

THE FIRST WEDDING IN THE FAMILY.

The great job of the cake-making over, a sense of leisure settled on the house. There seemed nothing left to be done which need put any one out of his or her way particularly. Katy had among her other qualities a great deal of what is called "forehandedness." To leave things to be attended to at the last moment in a flurry and a hurry would have been intolerable to her. She firmly believed in the doctrine of a certain wise man of our own day who says that to push your work before you is easy enough, but to pull it after you is very hard indeed.

All that winter, without saying much about it,—for Katy did not "do her thinking outside her head,"—she had been gradually making ready for the great event of the spring. Little by little, a touch here and a touch there, matters had been put in train, and the result now appeared in a surprising ease of mind and absence of confusion. The house had received its spring cleaning a fortnight earlier than usual, and was in fair, nice order, with freshly-beaten carpets and newly-washed curtains. Katy's dresses were ordered betimes, and had come home, been tried on, and folded away ten days before the wedding. They were not many in number, but all were pretty and in good taste, for the frigate was to be in Bar Harbor and Newport for a part of the summer, and Katy wanted to do Ned credit, and look well in his eyes and those of his friends.

All the arrangements, kept studiously simple, were beautifully systematized; and their very simplicity made them easy to carry out. The guest chambers were completely ready, one or two extra helpers were engaged that the servants might not be overworked, the order of every meal for the three busiest days was settled and written down. Each of the younger sisters had some special charge committed to her. Elsie was to wait on Cousin Helen, and see that she and her nurse had everything they wanted. Clover was to care for the two Roses; Johnnie to oversee the table arrangements, and make sure that all was right in that direction. Dear little Amy was indefatigable as a doer of errands, and her quick feet were at everybody's service to "save steps." Cecy arrived, and haunted the house all day long, anxious to be of use to somebody; Mrs. Ashe put her time at their disposal; there was such a superabundance of helpers, in fact, that no one could feel over taxed. And Katy, while still serving as main spring to the whole, had plenty of time to write her notes, open her wedding presents, and enjoy her friends in a leisurely, unfatigued fashion which was a standing wonderment to Cecy, whose own wedding had been of the onerous sort, and had worn her to skin and bone.

"I am only just beginning to recover from it now," she remarked plaintively, "and there you sit, Katy, looking as fresh as a rose; not tired a bit, and never seeming to have anything on your mind. I can't think how you do it. I never was at a wedding before where everybody was not perfectly worn out."

"You never were at such a simple wedding before," explained Katy. "I'm not ambitious, you see. I want to keep things pretty much as they are every day, only with a little more of everything because of there being more people to provide for. If I were attempting to make it a beautiful, picturesque wedding, we should get as tired as anybody, I have no doubt."

Katy's gifts were numerous enough to satisfy even Clover, and comprised all manner of things, from a silver tray which came, with a rather stiff note, from Mrs. Page and Lilly, to Mary's new flour-scoop, Debby's sifter, and a bottle of home-made hair tonic from an old woman in the "County Home." Each of the brothers and sisters had made her something, Katy having expressed a preference for presents of home manufacture. Mrs. Ashe gave her a beautiful sapphire ring, and Cecy Hall—as they still called her inadvertently half the time—an elaborate sofa-pillow embroidered by herself. Katy liked all her gifts, both large and small, both for what they were and for what they meant, and took a good healthy, hearty satisfaction in the fact that so many people cared for her, and had worked to give her a pleasure.

Cousin Helen was the first guest to arrive, five days before the wedding. When Dr. Carr, who had gone to Buffalo to meet and escort her down, lifted her from the carriage and carried her indoors, all of them could easily have fancied that it was the first visit happening over again, for she looked exactly as she did then, and scarcely a day older. She happened to have on a soft gray travelling dress too, much like that which she wore on the previous occasion, which made the illusion more complete.

But there was no illusion to Cousin Helen herself. Everything to her seemed changed and quite different. The ten years which had passed so lightly over her head had made a vast alteration in the cousins whom she remembered as children. The older ones were grown up, the younger ones in a fair way to be so; even Phil, who had been in white frocks with curls falling over his shoulders at the time of her former visit to Burnet, was now fifteen and as tall as his father. He was very slight in build, and looked delicate, she thought; but Katy assured her that he was perfectly well, and thin only because he had outgrown his strength.

It was one of the delightful results of Katy's "forehandedness" that she could command time during those next two days to thoroughly enjoy Cousin Helen. She sat beside her sofa for hours at a time, holding her hand and talking with a freedom of confidence such as she could have shown to no one else, except perhaps to Clover. She had the feeling that in so doing she was rendering account to a sort of visible conscience of all the events, the mistakes, the successes, the glad and the sorry of the long interval that had passed since they met. It was a pleasure and relief to her; and to Cousin Helen the recital was of equal interest, for though she knew the main facts by letter, there was a satisfaction in collecting the little details which seldom get fully put into letters.

One subject only Katy touched rather guardedly; and that was Ned. She was so desirous that her cousin should approve of him, and so anxious not to raise her expectations and have her disappointed, that she would not half say how very nice she herself thought him to be. But Cousin Helen could "read between the lines," and out of Katy's very reserve she constructed an idea of Ned which satisfied her pretty well.

So the two happy days passed, and on the third arrived the other anxiously expected guests, Rose Red and little Rose.

They came early in the morning, when no one was particularly looking for them, which made it all the pleasanter. Clover was on the porch twisting the honeysuckle tendrils upon the trellis when the carriage drove up to the gate, and Rose's sunny face popped out of the window. Clover recognized her at once, and with a shriek which brought all the others downstairs, flew down the path, and had little Rose in her arms before any one else could get there.

"You see before you a deserted wife," was Rose's first salutation. "Deniston has just dumped us on the wharf, and gone on to Chicago in that abominable boat, leaving me to your tender mercies. O Business, Business! what crimes are committed in thy name, as Madame Roland would say!"

"Never mind Deniston," cried Clover, with a rapturous squeeze. "Let us play that he doesn't exist, for a little while. We have got you now, and we mean to keep you."

"How pleasant you look!" said Rose, glancing up the locust walk toward the house, which wore a most inviting and hospitable air, with doors and windows wide open, and the soft wind fluttering the vines and the white curtains. "Ah, there comes Katy now." She ran forward to meet her while Clover followed with little Rose.

"Let me det down, pease," said that young lady,—the first remark she had made. "I tan walk all by myself. I am not a baby any more."

"*Will* you hear her talk?" cried Katy, catching her up. "Isn't it wonderful? Rosebud, who am I, do you think?"

"My Aunt Taty, I dess, betause you is so big. Is you mawwied yet?"

"No, indeed. Did you think I would get 'mawwied' without you? I have been waiting for you and mamma to come and help me."

"Well, we is here," in a tone of immense satisfaction. "Now you tan."

The larger Rose meanwhile was making acquaintance with the others. She needed no introductions, but seemed to know by instinct which was each boy and each girl, and to fit the right names to them all. In five minutes she seemed as much at home as though she had spent her life in Burnet. They bore her into the house in a sort of triumph, and upstairs to the blue bedroom, which Katy and Clover had vacated for her; and such a hubbub of talk and laughter presently issued therefrom that Cousin Helen, on the other side the entry, asked Jane to set her door open that she might enjoy the sounds,—they were so merry.

Rose's bright, rather high-pitched voice was easily distinguishable above the rest. She was evidently relating some experience of her journey, with an occasional splash by way of accompaniment, which suggested that she might be washing her hands.

"Yes, she really has grown awfully pretty; and she had on the loveliest dark-brown suit you ever saw, with a fawn-colored hat, and was altogether dazzling;

and, do you know, I was really quite glad to see her. I can't imagine why, but I was! I didn't stay glad long, however."

"Why not? What did she do?" This in Clover's voice.

"Well, she didn't do anything, but she was distant and disagreeable. I scarcely observed it at first, I was so pleased to see one of the old Hillsover girls; and I went on being very cordial. Then Lilly tried to put me down by running over a list of her fine acquaintances, Lady this, and the Marquis of that,—people whom she and her mother had known abroad. It made me think of my old autograph book with Antonio de Vallombrosa, and the rest. Do you remember?"

"Of course we do. Well, go on."

"At last she said something about Comte Ernest de Conflans,—I had heard of him, perhaps? He crossed in the steamer with 'Mamma and me,' it seems; and we have seen a great deal of him. This appeared a good opportunity to show that I too have relations with the nobility, so I said yes, I had met him in Boston, and my sister had seen a good deal of him in Washington last winter.

"'And what did she think of him?' demanded Lilly.

"'Well,' said I, 'she didn't seem to think a great deal about him. She says all the young men at the French legation seem more than usually foolish, but Comte Ernest is the worst of the lot. He really *does* look like an absolute fool, you know,' I added pleasantly. Now, girls, what was there in that to make her angry? Can you tell? She grew scarlet, and glared as if she wanted to bite my head off; and then she turned her back and would scarcely speak to me again. Does she always behave that way when the aristocracy is lightly spoken of?"

"Oh, Rose,—oh, Rose," cried Clover, in fits of laughter, "did you really tell her that?"

"I really did. Why shouldn't I? Is there any reason in particular?"

"Only that she is engaged to him," replied Katy, in an extinguished voice.

"Good gracious! No wonder she scowled! This is really dreadful. But then why did she look so black when she asked where we were going, and I said to your wedding? That didn't seem to please her any more than my little remarks about the nobility."

"I don't pretend to understand Lilly," said Katy, temperately; "she is an odd girl."

"I suppose an odd girl can't be expected to have an even temper," remarked Rose, apparently speaking with a hairpin in her mouth. "Well, I've done for myself, that is evident. I need never expect any notice in future from the Comtesse de Conflans."

Cousin Helen heard no more, but presently steps sounded outside her door, and Katy looked in to ask if she were dressed, and if she might bring Rose in, a request which was gladly granted. It was a pretty sight to see Rose with Cousin Helen. She knew all about her already from Clover and Katy, and fell at once under the gentle spell which seemed always to surround that invalid sofa, begged leave to say "Cousin Helen" as the others did, and was altogether at her best and sweetest when with her, full of merriment, but full too of a deference and sympathy which made her particularly charming.

"I never did see anything so lovely in all my life before," she told Clover in confidence. "To watch her lying there looking so radiant and so peaceful and so interested in Katy's affairs, and never once seeming to remember that except for that accident she too would have been a bride and had a wedding! It's perfectly wonderful! Do you suppose she is never sorry for herself? She seems the merriest of us all."

"I don't think she remembers herself often enough to be sorry. She is always thinking of some one else, it seems to me."

"Well, I am glad to have seen her," added Rose, in a more serious tone than was usual to her. "She and grandmamma are of a different order of beings from the rest of the world. I don't wonder you and Katy always were so good; you ought to be with such a Cousin Helen."

"I don't think we were as good as you make us out, but Cousin Helen has really been one of the strong influences of our lives. She was the making of Katy, when she had that long illness; and Katy has made the rest of us."

Little Rose from the first moment became the delight of the household, and especially of Amy Ashe, who could not do enough for her, and took her off her mother's hands so entirely that Rose complained that she seemed to have lost her child as well as her husband. She was a sedate little maiden, and wonderfully wise for her years. Already, in some ways she seemed older than her erratic little mother, of whom, in a droll fashion, she assumed a sort of charge. She was a born housewife.

"Mamma, you have fordotten your wings," Clover would hear her saying. "Mamma, you has a wip in your seeve, you must mend it," or "Mamma, don't fordet dat your teys is in the top dwawer,"—all these reminders and advices being made particularly comical by the baby pronunciation. Rose's theory was that little Rose was a messenger from heaven sent to buffet her and correct her mistakes.

"The bane and the antidote," she would say. "Think of my having a child with powers of ratiocination!"

Rose came down the night of her arrival after a long, freshening nap, looking rested and bonny in a pretty blue dress, and saying that as little Rose too had taken a good sleep, she might sit up to tea if the family liked. The family were only too pleased to have her do so. After tea Rose carried her off, ostensibly to go to bed, but Clover heard a great deal of confabulating and giggling in the hall and on the stairs, and soon after, Rose returned, the door-bell rang loudly, and there entered an astonishing vision,—little Rose, costumed as a Cupid or a carrier-pigeon, no one knew exactly which, with a pair of large white wings fastened on her shoulders, and dragging behind her by a loop of ribbon a sizeable basket quite full of parcels.

Straight toward Katy she went, and with her small hands behind her back and her blue eyes fixed full on Katy's face, repeated with the utmost solemnity the following "poem:"

"I'm a messender, you see,
Fwom Hymen's Expwess Tumpany.
All these little bundles are
For my Aunty Taty Tarr;
If she knows wot's dood for her
She will tiss the messender."

"You sweet thing!" cried Katy, "tissing the messender" with all her heart. "I never heard such a dear little poem. Did you write it yourself, Roslein?"

"No. Mamma wote it, but she teached it to me so I tould say it."

The bundles of course contained wedding gifts. Rose seemed to have brought her trunk full of them. There were a pretty pair of salt-cellars from Mrs. Redding, a charming paper-knife of silver, with an antique coin set in the handle, from Sylvia, a hand-mirror mounted in brass from Esther Dearborn, a long towel with fringed and embroidered ends from Ellen Gray, and from dear old Mrs. Redding a beautiful lace-pin set with a moonstone. Next came a little *repoussé* pitcher marked, "With love from Mary Silver," then a parcel tied with pink ribbons, containing a card-case of Japanese leather, which was little Rose's gift, and last of all Rose's own present, a delightful case full of ivory brushes and combs. Altogether never was such a satisfactory "fardel" brought by Hymen's or any other express company before; and in opening the packages, reading the notes that came with them and exclaiming and admiring, time flew so fast that Rose quite forgot the hour, till little Rose, growing sleepy, reminded her of it by saying,—

"Mamma, I dess I'd better do to bed now, betause if I don't I shall be too seepy to turn to Aunt Taty's wedding to-mowwow."

"Dear me!" cried Rose, catching the child up. "This is simply dreadful! what a mother I am! Things *are* come to a pass indeed, if babes and sucklings have to ask to be put to bed. Baby, you ought to have been christened Nathan the Wise."

She disappeared with Roslein's drowsy eyes looking over her shoulder.

Next afternoon came Ned, and with him, to Katy's surprise and pleasure, appeared the good old commodore who had played such a kind part in their affairs in Italy the year before. It was a great compliment that he should think it worth while to come so far to see one of his junior officers married; and it showed so much real regard for Ned that everybody was delighted. These guests were quartered with Mrs. Ashe, but they took most of their meals with the Carrs; and it was arranged that they, with Polly and Amy, should come to an early breakfast on the marriage morning.

After Ned's arrival things did seem to grow a little fuller and busier, for he naturally wanted Katy to himself, and she was too preoccupied to keep her calm grasp on events; still all went smoothly, and Rose declared that there never was such a wedding since the world was made,—no tears, no worries, nobody looking tired, nothing disagreeable!

Clover's one great subject of concern was the fear that it might rain. There was a little haze about the sunset the night before, and she expressed her intention to Cousin Helen of lying awake all night to see how things looked.

"I really feel as if I could not bear it if it should storm," she said, "after all this fine weather too; and I know I shall not sleep a wink, anyway."

"I think we can trust God to take care of the weather even on Katy's wedding-day," replied Cousin Helen, gently.

And after all it was she who lay awake. Pain had made her a restless sleeper, and as her bed commanded the great arch of western sky, she saw the moon, a sharp-curved silver shape, descend and disappear a little before midnight. She roused again when all was still, solemn darkness except for a spangle of stars, and later, opened her eyes in time to catch the faint rose flush of dawn reflected from the east. She raised herself on her elbow to watch the light grow.

"It is a fair day for the child," she whispered to herself. "How good God is!" Then she slept again for a long, restful space, and woke refreshed, so that Katy's secret fear that Cousin Helen might be ill from excitement, and not able to come to her wedding, was not realized.

Clover, meantime, had slept soundly all night. She and Katy shared the same room, and waked almost at the same moment. It was early still; but the sisters felt bright and rested and ready for work, so they rose at once.

They dressed in silence, after a little whispered rejoicing over the beautiful morning, and in silence took their Bibles and sat down side by side to read the daily portion which was their habit. Then hand in hand they stole downstairs, disturbing nobody, softly opened doors and windows, carried bowls and jars out on the porch, and proceeded to arrange a great basket full of roses which had been brought the night before, and set in the dew-cool shade of the willows to keep fresh.

Before breakfast all the house had put on festal airs. Summer had come early to Burnet that year; every garden was in bud and blossom, and every one who had flowers had sent their best to grace Katy's wedding. The whole world seemed full of delicious smells. Each table and chimney-piece bore a fragrant load; a great bowl of Jacqueminots stood in the middle of the breakfast-table, and two large jars of the same on the porch, where Clover had arranged various seats and cushions that it might serve as a sort of outdoor parlor.

Nobody who came to that early breakfast ever forgot its peace and pleasantness and the sweet atmosphere of affection which seemed to pervade everything about it. After breakfast came family prayers as usual, Dr. Carr reading the chapter, and the dear old commodore joining with a hearty nautical voice in,—

"Awake my soul! and with the sun,"

which was a favorite hymn with all of them. Ned shared Katy's book, and his face and hers alone would have been breakfast enough for the company if everything else had failed, as Rose remarked to Clover in a whisper, though nobody found any fault with the more substantial fare which Debby had sent in previously. Somehow this little mutual service of prayer and praise seemed to fit in with the spirit of the day, and give it its keynote.

"It's just the sweetest wedding," Mrs. Ashe told her brother. "And the wonderful thing is that everything comes so naturally. Katy is precisely her usual self,—only a little more so."

"I'm under great obligations to Amy for having that fever," was Ned's somewhat indirect answer; but his sister understood what he meant.

Breakfast over, the guests discreetly removed themselves; and the whole family joined in resetting the table for the luncheon, which was to be at two, Katy and Ned departing in the boat at four. It was a simple but abundant repast, with plenty of delicious home-cooked food,—oysters and salads and cold chicken; fresh salmon from Lake Superior; a big Virginia ham baked to perfection, red and translucent to its savory centre; hot coffee, and quantities of Debby's perfect rolls. There were strawberries, also, and ice-cream, and the best of home-made cake and jellies, and everywhere vases of fresh roses to perfume the feast. When all was arranged, there was still time for Katy to make Cousin Helen a visit, and then go to her room for a quiet rest before dressing; and still that same unhurried air pervaded the house.

There had been a little discussion the night before as to just how the bride should make her appearance at the decisive moment; but Katy had settled it by saying simply that she should come downstairs, and Ned could meet her at the foot of the staircase.

"It is the simplest way," she said; "and you know I don't want any fuss. I will just come down."

"I dare say she's right," remarked Rose; "but it seems to me to require a great deal of courage."

And after all, it didn't. The simple and natural way of doing a thing generally turns out the easiest. Clover helped Katy to put on the wedding-gown of soft crape and creamy white silk. It was trimmed with old lace and knots of ribbon, and Katy wore with it two or three white roses which Ned had brought her, and a pearl pendant which was his gift. Then Clover had to go downstairs to receive the guests, and see that Cousin Helen's sofa was put in the right place; and Rose, who remained behind, had the pleasure of arranging Katy's veil. The yellow-white of the old blonde was very becoming, and altogether, the effect, though not "stylish," was very sweet. Katy was a little pale, but otherwise exactly like her usual self, with no tremors or self-consciousness.

Presently little Rose came up with a message.

"Aunty Tover says dat Dr. Tone has tum, and everything is weddy, and you'd better tum down," she announced.

Katy gave Rose a last kiss, and went down the hall. But little Rose was so fascinated by the appearance of the white dress and veil that she kept fast hold of Katy's hand, disregarding her mother's suggestion that she should slip down the back staircase, as she herself proposed to do.

"No, I want to do with my Aunt Taty," she persisted.

So it chanced that Katy came downstairs with pretty little Rose clinging to her like a sort of impromptu bridesmaid; and meeting Ned's eyes as he stood at the foot waiting for her, she forgot herself, lost the little sense of shyness which was creeping over her, and responded to his look with a tender, brilliant smile. The light from the hall-door caught her face and figure just then, the color flashed into her cheeks; and she looked like a beautiful, happy picture of a bride, and all by accident,—which was the best thing about it; for pre-arranged effects are not always effective, and are apt to betray their pre-arrangement.

Then Katy took Ned's arm, little Rose let go her hand, and they went into the parlor and were married.

Dr. Stone had an old-fashioned and very solemn wedding service which he was accustomed to use on such occasions. He generally spoke of the bride as "Thy handmaiden," which was a form that Clover particularly deprecated. He had also been known to advert to the world where there is neither marrying nor giving in marriage as a great improvement on this, which seemed, to say the least, an unfortunate allusion under the circumstances. But upon this occasion his feelings were warmed and touched, and he called Katy "My dear child," which was much better than "Thy handmaiden."

When the ceremony was over, Ned kissed Katy, and her father kissed her, and the girls and Dorry and Phil; and then, without waiting for any one else, she left her place and went straight to where Cousin Helen lay on her sofa, watching the scene with those clear, tender eyes in which no shadow of past regrets could be detected. Katy knelt down beside her, and they exchanged a long, silent embrace. There was no need for words between hearts which knew each other so well.

After that for a little while all was congratulations and good wishes. I think no bride ever carried more hearty good-will into her new life than did my Katy. All sorts of people took Ned off into corners to tell him privately what a fortunate person he was in winning such a wife. Each fresh confidence of this sort was a fresh delight to him, he so thoroughly agreed with it.

"She's a prize, sir!—she's a prize!" old Mr. Worrett kept repeating, shaking Ned's hand with each repetition. Mrs. Worrett had not been able to come. She never left home now on account of the prevailing weakness of carryalls; but she sent Katy her best love and a gorgeous broom made of the tails of her own peacocks.

"Aren't you sorry you are not going to stay and have a nice time with us all, and help eat up the rest of the cake?" demanded Clover, as she put her head into the carriage for a last kiss, two hours later.

"Very!" said Katy; but she didn't look sorry at all.

"There's one comfort," Clover remarked valiantly, as she walked back to the house with her arm round Rose's waist. "She's coming back in December, when the ship sails, and as likely as not she will stay a year, or perhaps two. That's what I like about the navy. You can eat your cake, and have it too. Husbands go off for good long times, and leave their wives behind them. I think it's delightful!"

"I wonder if Katy will think it quite so delightful," remarked Rose. "Girls are not always so anxious to ship their husbands off for what you call 'good long times.'"

"I think she ought. It seems to me perfectly unnatural that any one should want to leave her own family and go away for always. I like Ned dearly, but except for this blessed arrangement about going to sea, I don't see how Katy could."

"Clover, you are a goose. You'll be wiser one of these days, see if you aren't," was Rose's only reply.

CHAPTER IV.

TWO LONG YEARS IN ONE SHORT CHAPTER.

Katy's absence left a sad blank in the household. Every one missed her, but nobody so much as Clover, who all her life long had been her room-mate, confidante, and intimate friend.

It was a great help that Rose was there for the first three lonely days. Dulness and sadness were impossible with that vivacious little person at hand; and so long as she stayed, Clover had small leisure to be mournful. Rose was so bright and merry and affectionate that Elsie and John were almost as much in love with her as Clover herself, and sat and sunned themselves in her warmth, so to speak, all day long, while Phil and Dorry fairly quarrelled as to which should have the pleasure of doing little services for her and Baby Rose.

If she could have remained the summer through, all would have seemed easy; but that of course was impossible. Mr. Browne appeared with a provoking punctuality on the morning of the fourth day, prepared to carry his family away with him. He spent one night at Dr. Carr's, and they all liked him very much. No one could help it, he was so cordial and friendly and pleasant. Still, for all her liking, Clover could have found it in her heart to quite detest him as the final moment drew near.

"Let him go home without you," she urged coaxingly. "Stay with us all summer,—you and little Rose! He can come back in September to fetch you, and it would be so delightful to us."

"My dear, I couldn't live without Deniston till September," said the disappointing Rose. "It may not show itself to a casual observer, but I am really quite foolish about Deniston. I shouldn't be happy away from him at all. He's the only husband I've got,—a 'poor thing, but mine own,' as the 'immortal William' puts it."

"Oh, dear," groaned Clover. "That is the way that Katy is going to talk about Ned, I suppose. Matrimony is the most aggravating condition of things for outsiders that was ever invented. I wish nobody *had* invented it. Here it would be so nice for us to have you stay, and the moment that provoking husband of yours appears, you can't think of any one else."

"Too true—much too true. Now, Clovy, don't embitter our last moments with reproaches. It's hard enough to leave you as it is, when I've just found you again after all these years. I've had the most beautiful visit that ever was, and you've all been awfully dear and nice. 'Kiss me quick and let me go,' as the song says. I only wish Burnet was next door to West Cedar Street!"

Next day Mr. Browne sailed away with his "handful of Roses," as Elsie sentimentally termed them (and indeed, Rose by herself would have been a handful for almost any man); and Clover, like Lord Ullin, was "left lamenting." Cousin Helen remained, however; and it was not till she too departed, a week later, that Clover fully recognized what it meant to have Katy married. Then indeed she could have found it in her heart to emulate Eugénie de la Ferronayes, and shed tears over all the little inanimate objects which her sister had left behind,—the worn-out gloves, the old dressing slippers in the shoe-bag. But dear me, we get used to everything, and it is fortunate that we do! Life is too full, and hearts too flexible, and really sad things too sad, for the survival of sentimental regrets over changes which do not involve real loss and the wide separation of death. In time, Clover learned to live without Katy, and to be cheerful still.

Her cheerfulness was greatly helped by the letters which came regularly, and showed how contented Katy herself was. She and Ned were having a beautiful time, first in New York, and making visits near it, then in Portsmouth and Portland, when the frigate moved on to these harbors, and in Newport, which was full and gay and amusing to the last degree. Later, in August, the letters came from Bar Harbor, where Katy had followed, in company with the commodore's wife, who seemed as nice as her husband; and Clover heard of all manner of delightful doings,—sails, excursions, receptions on board ship, and long moonlight paddles with Ned, who was an expert canoeist. Everybody was so wonderfully kind, Katy said; but Ned wrote to his sister that Katy was a great favorite; every one liked her, and his particular friends were all raging wildly round in quest of girls just like her to marry. "But it's no use; for, as I tell them," he added, "that sort isn't made in batches. There is only one Katy; and happily she belongs to me, and the other fellows must get along as they can."

This was all satisfactory and comforting; and Clover could endure a little loneliness herself so long as her beloved Katy seemed so happy. She was very busy besides, and there *were* compensations, as she admitted to herself. She liked the consequence of being at the head of domestic affairs, and succeeding to Katy's position as papa's special daughter,—the person to whom he came for all he wanted, and to whom he told his little secrets. She and Elsie became more intimate than they had ever been before; and Elsie in her turn enjoyed being Clover's lieutenant as Clover had been Katy's. So the summer did not seem long to any of them; and when September was once past, and they could begin to say, "month after next," the time sped much faster.

"Mrs. Hall asked me this morning when the Worthingtons were coming," said Johnnie, one day. "It seems so funny to have Katy spoken of as 'the Worthingtons.'"

"I only wish the Worthingtons would write and say when," remarked Clover. "It is more than a week since we heard from them."

The next day brought the wished-for letter, and the good news that Ned had a fortnight's leave, and meant to bring Katy home the middle of November, and stay for Thanksgiving. After that the "Natchitoches" was to sail for an eighteen months' cruise to China and Japan; and then Ned would probably have two years ashore at the Torpedo Station or Naval Academy or somewhere, and they would start a little home for themselves.

"Meantime," wrote Katy, "I am coming to spend a year and a half with you, if urged. Don't all speak at once, and don't mind saying so, if you don't want me."

The bitter drop in this pleasant intelligence—there generally is one, you know—was that the fortnight of Ned's stay was to be spent at Mrs. Ashe's. "It's her only chance to see Ned," said Katy; "so I know you won't mind, for afterward you will have me for such a long visit."

But they *did* mind very much!

"I don't think it's fair," cried Johnnie, hotly, while Clover and Elsie exchanged disgusted looks; "Katy belongs to us."

"Katy belongs to her husband, on the contrary," said Dr. Carr, overhearing her; "you must learn that lesson once for all, children. There's no escape from the melancholy fact; and it's quite right and natural that Ned should wish to go to his sister, and she should want to have him."

"Ned! yes. But Katy—"

"My dear, Katy *is* Ned," answered Dr. Carr, with a twinkle. Then noticing the extremely unconvinced expression of Johnnie's face, he added more seriously, "Don't be cross, children, and spoil all Katy's pleasure in coming home, with your foolish jealousies. Clover, I trust to you to take these young mutineers in hand and make them listen to reason."

Thus appealed to, Clover rallied her powers, and while laboring to bring Elsie and John to a proper frame of mind, schooled herself as well, so as to be able to treat Mrs. Ashe amiably when they met. Dear, unconscious Polly meanwhile was devising all sorts of pleasant and hospitable plans designed to make Ned's stay a sort of continuous fête to everybody. She put on no airs over the preference shown her, and was altogether so kind and friendly and sweet that no one could quarrel with her even in thought, and Johnnie herself had to forgive her, and be contented with a little whispered grumble to Dorry now and then over the inconvenience of possessing "people-in-law."

And then Katy came, the same Katy, only, as Clover thought, nicer, brighter, dearer, and certainly better-looking than ever. Sea air had tanned her a little, but the brown was becoming; and she had gained an ease and polish of manner which her sisters admired very much. And after all, it seemed to make little difference at which house they stayed, for they were in and out of both all day long; and Mrs. Ashe threw her doors open to the Carrs and wanted some or all of them for every meal, so that except for the name of the thing, it was almost as satisfactory to have Katy over the way as occupying her old quarters.

The fortnight sped only too rapidly. Ned departed, and Katy settled herself in the familiar corner to wait till he should come back again. Navy wives have to learn the hard lesson of patience in the long separations entailed by their husbands' profession. Katy missed Ned sorely, but she was too unselfish to mope, or to let the others know how hard to bear his loss seemed to her. She never told any one how she lay awake in stormy nights, or when the wind blew,—and it seemed to blow oftener than usual that winter,—imagining the frigate in a gale, and whispering little prayers for Ned's safety. Then her good sense would come back, and remind her that wind in Burnet did not necessarily mean wind in Shanghai or Yokohama or wherever the "Natchitoches" might be; and she would put herself to sleep with the repetition of that lovely verse of

Keble's "Evening Hymn," left out in most of the collections, but which was particularly dear to her:—

"Thou Ruler of the light and dark,
  Guide through the tempest Thine own Ark;
  Amid the howling, wintry sea,
  We are in port if we have Thee."

So the winter passed, and the spring; and another summer came and went, with little change to the quiet Burnet household, and Katy's brief life with her husband began to seem dreamy and unreal, it lay so far behind. And then, with the beginning of the second winter came a new anxiety.

Phil, as we said in the last chapter, had grown too fast to be very strong, and was the most delicate of the family in looks and health, though full of spirit and fun. Going out to skate with some other boys the week before Christmas, on a pond which was not so securely frozen as it looked, the ice gave way; and though no one was drowned, the whole party had a drenching, and were thoroughly chilled. None of the others minded it much, but the exposure had a serious effect on Phil. He caught a bad cold which rapidly increased into pneumonia; and Christmas Day, usually such a bright one in the Carr household, was overshadowed by anxious forebodings, for Phil was seriously ill, and the doctor felt by no means sure how things would turn with him. The sisters nursed him devotedly, and by March he was out again; but he did not get *well* or lose the persistent little cough, which kept him thin and weak. Dr. Carr tried this remedy and that, but nothing seemed to do much good; and Katy thought that her father looked graver and more anxious every time that he tested Phil's temperature or listened at his chest.

"It's not serious yet," he told her in private; "but I don't like the look of things. The boy is just at a turning-point. Any little thing might set him one way or the other. I wish I could send him away from this damp lake climate."

But sending a half-sick boy away is not such an easy thing, nor was it quite clear where he ought to go. So matters drifted along for another month, and then Phil settled the question for himself by having a slight hemorrhage. It was evident that something must be done, and speedily—but what? Dr. Carr wrote to various medical acquaintances, and in reply pamphlets and letters poured in, each designed to prove that the particular part of the country to which the pamphlet or the letter referred was the only one to which it was at all worth while to consign an invalid with delicate lungs. One recommended Florida, another Georgia, a third South Carolina; a fourth and fifth recommended cold instead of heat, and an open air life with the mercury at zero. It was hard to decide what was best.

"He ought not to go off alone either," said the puzzled father. "He is neither old enough nor wise enough to manage by himself, but who to send with him is the puzzle. It doubles the expense, too."

"Perhaps I—" began Katy, but her father cut her short with a gesture.

"No, Katy, I couldn't permit that. Your husband is due in a few weeks now. You must be free to go to him wherever he is, not hampered with the care of a sick brother. Besides, whoever takes charge of Phil must be prepared for a long absence,—at least a year. It must be either Clover or myself; and as it seems out of the question that I shall drop my practice for a year, Clover is the person."

"Phil is seventeen now," suggested Katy. "That is not so very young."

"No, not if he were in full health. Plenty of boys no older than he have gone out West by themselves, and fared perfectly well. But in Phil's condition that would never answer. He has a tendency to be low-spirited about himself too, and he needs incessant care and watchfulness."

"Out West," repeated Katy. "Have you decided, then?"

"Yes. The letter I had yesterday from Hope, makes me pretty sure that St. Helen's is the best place we have heard of."

"St. Helen's! Where is that?"

"It is one of the new health-resorts in Colorado which has lately come into notice for consumptives. It's very high up; nearly or quite six thousand feet, and the air is said to be something remarkable."

"Clover will manage beautifully, I think; she is such a sensible little thing," said Katy.

"She seems to me, and he too, about as fit to go off two thousand miles by themselves as the Babes in the Wood," remarked Dr. Carr, who, like many other fathers, found it hard to realize that his children had outgrown their childhood. "However, there's no help for it. If I don't stay and grind away at the mill, there is no one to pay for this long journey. Clover will have to do her best."

"And a very good best it will be you'll see," said Katy, consolingly. "Does Dr. Hope tell you anything about the place?" she added, turning over the letter which her father had handed her.

"Oh, he says the scenery is fine, and the mean rain-fall is this, and the mean precipitation that, and that boarding-places can be had. That is pretty much all. So far as climate goes, it is the right place, but I presume the accommodations are poor enough. The children must go prepared to rough it. The town was only settled ten or eleven years ago; there hasn't been time to make things comfortable," remarked Dr. Carr, with a truly Eastern ignorance of the rapid way in which things march in the far West.

Clover's feelings when the decision was announced to her it would be hard to explain in full. She was both confused and exhilarated by the sudden weight of responsibility laid upon her. To leave everybody and everything she had always been used to, and go away to such a distance alone with Phil, made her gasp with a sense of dismay, while at the same time the idea that for the first time in her life she was trusted with something really important, roused her energies, and made her feel braced and valiant, like a soldier to whom some difficult enterprise is intrusted on the day of battle.

Many consultations followed as to what the travellers should carry with them, by what route they would best go, and how prepare for the journey. A great deal of contradictory advice was offered, as is usually the case when people are starting on a voyage or a long railway ride. One friend wrote to recommend that they should provide themselves with a week's provisions in advance, and enclosed a list of crackers, jam, potted meats, tea, fruit, and hardware, which would have made a heavy load for a donkey or mule to carry. How were poor Clover and Phil to transport such a weight of things? Another advised against umbrellas and water-proof cloaks,—what was the use of such things where it never rained?—while a second letter, received the same day, assured them that thunder and hail storms were things for which travellers in Colorado must live in a state of continual preparation. "Who shall decide when doctors disagree?" In the end Clover concluded that it was best to follow the leadings of commonsense and rational precaution, do about a quarter of what people advised, and leave the rest undone; and she found that this worked very well.

As they knew so little of the resources of St. Helen's, and there was such a strong impression prevailing in the family as to its being a rough sort of newly-settled place, Clover and Katy judged it wise to pack a large box of stores to go out by freight: oatmeal and arrowroot and beef-extract and Albert biscuits,—things which Philly ought to have, and which in a wild region might be hard to come by. Debby filled all the corners with home-made dainties of various sorts; and Clover, besides a spirit-lamp and a tea-pot, put into her trunks various small decorations,—Japanese fans and pictures, photographs, a vase or two, books and a sofa-pillow,—things which took little room, and which she thought would make their quarters look more comfortable in case they were very bare and unfurnished. People felt sorry for the probable hardships the brother and sister were to undergo; and they had as many little gifts and notes of sympathy and counsel as Katy herself when she was starting for Europe.

But I am anticipating. Before the trunks were packed, Dr. Carr's anxieties about his "Babes in the Wood" were greatly allayed by a visit from Mrs. Hall. She came to tell him that she had heard of a possible "matron" for Clover.

"I am not acquainted with the lady myself," she said; "but my cousin, who writes about her, knows her quite well, and says she is a highly respectable person, and belongs to nice people. Her sister, or some one, married a Phillips of Boston, and I've always heard that that family was one of the best there. She's had some malarial trouble, and is at the West now on account of it, staying with a friend in Omaha; but she wants to spend the summer at St. Helen's. And as I know you have worried a good deal over having Clover and Phil go off by themselves, I thought it might be a comfort to you to hear of this Mrs. Watson."

"You are very good. If she proves to be the right sort of person, it *will* be an immense comfort. Do you know when she wants to start?"

"About the end of May,—just the right time, you see. She could join Clover and Philip as they go through, which will work nicely for them all."

"So it will. Well, this is quite a relief. Please write to your cousin, Mrs. Hall, and make the arrangement. I don't want Mrs. Watson to be burdened with any real care of the children, of course; but if she can arrange to go along with them, and give Clover a word of advice now and then, should she need it, I shall be easier in my mind about them."

Clover was only doubtfully grateful when she heard of this arrangement.

"Papa always will persist in thinking that I am a baby still," she said to Katy, drawing her little figure up to look as tall as possible. "I am twenty-two, I would have him remember. How do we know what this Mrs. Watson is like? She may be the most disagreeable person in the world for all papa can tell."

"I really can't find it in my heart to be sorry that it has happened, papa looks so much relieved by it," Katy rejoined.

But all dissatisfactions and worries and misgivings took wings and flew away when, just ten days before the travellers were to start, a new and delightful change was made in the programme. Ned telegraphed that the ship, instead of coming to New York, was ordered to San Francisco to refit, and he wanted Katy to join him there early in June, prepared to spend the summer; while almost simultaneously came a letter from Mrs. Ashe, who with Amy had been staying a couple of months in New York, to say that hearing of Ned's plan had decided her also to take a trip to California with some friends who had previously asked her to join them. These friends were, it seemed, the Daytons of Albany. Mr. Dayton was a railroad magnate, and had the control of a private car in which the party were to travel; and Mrs. Ashe was authorized to invite Katy, and Clover and Phil also, to go along with them,—the former all the way to California, and the others as far as Denver, where the roads separated.

This was truly delightful. Such an offer was surely worth a few days' delay. The plan seemed to settle itself all in one minute. Mrs. Watson, whom every one now regretted as a complication, was the only difficulty; but a couple of telegrams settled that perplexity, and it was arranged that she should join them on the same train, though in a different car. To have Katy as a fellow-traveller, and Mrs. Ashe and Amy, made a different thing of the long journey, and Clover proceeded with her preparations in jubilant spirits.

CHAPTER V.

CAR FORTY-SEVEN.

It is they who stay behind who suffer most from leave-takings. Those who go have the continual change of scenes and impressions to help them to forget; those who remain must bear as best they may the dull heavy sense of loss and separation.

The parting at Burnet was not a cheerful one. Clover was oppressed with the nearness of untried responsibilities; and though she kept up a brave face, she was inwardly homesick. Phil slept badly the night before the start, and looked so wan and thin as he stood on the steamer's deck beside his sisters, waving good-by to the party on the wharf, that a new and sharp thrill of anxiety shot through his father's heart. The boy looked so young and helpless to be sent away ill among strangers, and round-faced little Clover seemed such a fragile support! There was no help for it. The thing was decided on, decided for the best, as they all hoped; but Dr. Carr was not at all happy in his mind as he watched the steamer become a gradually lessening speck in the distance, and he sighed heavily when at last he turned away.

Elsie echoed the sigh. She, too, had noticed Phil's looks and papa's gravity, and her heart felt heavy within her. The house, when they reached it, seemed lonely and empty. Papa went at once to his office, and they heard him lock the door. This was such an unusual proceeding in the middle of the morning that she and Johnnie opened wide eyes of dismay at each other.

"Is papa crying, do you suppose?" whispered John.

"No, I don't think it can be *that*. Papa never does cry; but I'm afraid he's feeling badly," responded Elsie, in the same hushed tone. "Oh, dear, how horrid it is not even to have Clover at home! What *are* we going to do without her and Katy?"

"I don't know I'm sure. You can't think how queer I feel, Elsie,—just as if my heart had slipped out of its place, and was going down, down into my boots. I think it must be the way people feel when they are homesick. I had it once before when I was at Inches Mills, but never since then. How I wish Philly had never gone to skate on that nasty pond!" and John burst into a passion of tears.

"Oh, don't, don't!" cried poor Elsie, for Johnnie's sobs were infectious, and she felt an ominous lump coming into her own throat, "don't behave so, Johnnie. Think if papa came out, and found us crying! Clover particularly said that we must make the house bright for him. I'm going to sow the mignonette seed [desperately]; come and help me. The trowel is on the back porch, and you might get Dorry's jack-knife and cut some little sticks to mark the places."

This expedient was successful. Johnnie, who loved to "whittle" above all things, dried her tears, and ran for her shade hat; and by the time the tiny brown seeds were sprinkled into the brown earth of the borders, both the girls were themselves again. Dr. Carr appeared from his retirement half an hour later. A note had come for him meanwhile, but somehow no one had quite liked to knock at the door and deliver it.

Elsie handed it to him now, with a timid, anxious look, whose import seemed to strike him, for he laughed a little, and pinched her cheek as he read.

"I've been writing to Dr. Hope about the children," he said; "that's all. Don't wait dinner for me, chicks. I'm off for the Corners to see a boy who's had a fall, and I'll get a bite there. Order something good for tea, Elsie; and afterward we'll have a game of cribbage if I'm not called out. We must be as jolly as we can, or Clover will scold us when she comes back."

Meanwhile the three travellers were faring through the first stage of their journey very comfortably. The fresh air and change brightened Phil; he ate a good dinner, and afterward took quite a long nap on a sofa, Clover sitting by to keep him covered and see that he did not get cold. Late in the evening they changed to the express train, and there again, Phil, after being tucked up behind the curtains of his section, went to sleep and passed a satisfactory night, so that he reached Chicago looking so much better than when they left Burnet that his father's heart would have been lightened could he have seen him.

Mrs. Ashe came down to the station to meet them, together with Mr. Dayton,—a kind, friendly man with a tired but particularly pleasant face. All the necessary transfer of baggage, etc., was made easy, and they were carried off at once to the hotel where rooms had been secured. There they were rapturously received by Amy, and introduced to Mrs. Dayton, a sweet, spirited little matron, with a face as kindly as her husband's, but not so worn. Mr. Dayton looked as if for years he had been bearing the whole weight of a railroad on his shoulders, as in one sense it may be said that he had.

"We have been here almost a whole day," said Amy, who had taken possession, as a matter of course, of her old perch on Katy's knee. "Chicago is the biggest place you ever saw, Tanta; but it isn't so pretty as Burnet. And oh! don't you think Car Forty-seven is nice,—the one we are going out West in, you know? And this morning Mr. Dayton took us to see it. It's the cunningest place that ever was. There's one dear little drawer in the wall that Mrs. Dayton says I may have to keep Mabel's things in. I never saw a drawer in a car before. There's a lovely little bedroom too, and such a nice washing-basin, and a kitchen, and all sorts of things. I can hardly wait till I show them to you. Don't you think that travelling is the most delightful thing in the world, Miss Clover?"

"Yes—if only—people—don't get too tired," said Clover, with an anxious glance at Phil, as he lay back in an easy-chair. She did not dare say, "if Phil doesn't get too tired," for she had already discovered that nothing annoyed him so much as being talked about as an invalid, and that he was very apt to revenge himself by doing something imprudent immediately afterward, to disguise from an observant world the fact that he couldn't do it without running a risk. Like most boys, he resented being "fussed over,"—a fact which made the care of him more difficult than it would otherwise have been.

The room which had been taken for Clover and Katy looked out on the lake, which was not far away; and the reach of blue water would have made a pretty view if trains of cars had not continually steamed between it and the hotel, staining the sky and blurring the prospect with their smokes. Katy wondered how it happened that the early settlers who laid out Chicago had not bethought themselves to secure this fine water frontage as an ornament to the future city; but Mr. Dayton explained that in the rapid growth of Western towns, things arranged themselves rather than were arranged for, and that the first pioneers had other things to think about than what a New Englander would call "sightliness,"—and Katy could easily believe this to be true.

Car Forty-seven was on the track when they drove to the station at noon next day. It was the end car of a long express train, which, Mr. Dayton told them, is considered the place of honor, and generally assigned to private cars. It was of an old-fashioned pattern, and did not compare, as they were informed, with the palaces on wheels built nowadays for the use of railroad presidents and directors. But though Katy heard of cars with French beds, plunge baths, open fireplaces, and other incredible luxuries, Car Forty-seven still seemed to her inexperienced eyes and Clover's a marvel of comfort and convenience.

A small kitchen, a store closet, and a sort of baggage-room, fitted with berths for two servants, occupied the end of the car nearest the engine. Then came a dressing-closet, with ample marble basins where hot water as well as cold was always on tap; then a wide state-room, with a bed on either side, and then a large compartment occupying the middle of the car, where by day four nice little dining-tables could be set, with a seat on either side, and by night six sleeping sections made up. The rest of the car was arranged as a sitting-room, glassed all around, and furnished with comfortable seats of various kinds, a writing-desk, two or three tables of different sizes, and various small lockers and receptacles, fitted into the partitions to serve as catch-alls for loose articles of all sorts.

Bunches of lovely roses and baskets of strawberries stood on the tables; and quite a number of the Daytons' friends had come down to see them off, each bringing some sort of good-by gift for the travellers,—flowers, hothouse grapes, early cherries, or home-made cake. They were all so cordial and pleasant and so interested in Phil, that Katy and Clover lost their hearts to each in turn, and forever afterward were ready to stand up for Chicago as the kindest place that ever was seen.

Then amid farewells and good wishes the train moved slowly out of the station, and the inmates of Car Forty-seven proceeded to "go to housekeeping," as Mrs. Dayton expressed it, and to settle themselves and their belongings in these new quarters. Mrs. Ashe and Amy, it was decided, should occupy the state-room, and the other ladies were to dress there when it was convenient. Sections were assigned to everybody,—Clover's opposite Phil's so that she might hear him if he needed anything in the night; and Mr. Dayton called for all the bonnets and hats, and amid much laughter proceeded to pin up each in thick folds of newspaper, and fasten it on a hook not to be taken down till the end of the journey. Mabel's feathered turban took its turn with the rest, at Amy's particular request. Dust was the main thing to be guarded against, and Katy, having been duly forewarned, had gone out in the morning, and bought for herself and

Clover soft hats of whity-gray felt and veils of the same color, like those which Mrs. Dayton and Polly had provided for the journey, and which had the advantage of being light as well as unspoilable.

But there was no dust that first morning, as the train ran smoothly across the fertile prairies of Illinois first, and then of Iowa, between fields dazzling with the fresh green of wheat and rye, and waysides studded with such wild-flowers as none of them had ever seen or dreamed of before. Pink spikes and white and vivid blue spikes; masses of brown and orange cups, like low-growing tulips; ranks of beautiful vetches and purple lupines; escholtzias, like immense sweeps of golden sunlight; wild sweet peas; trumpet-shaped blossoms whose name no one knew,—all flung broadcast over the face of the land, and in such stintless quantities that it dazzled the mind to think of as it did the eyes to behold them. The low-lying horizons looked infinitely far off; the sense of space was confusing. Here and there appeared a home-stead, backed with a "break-wind" of thickly-planted trees; but the general impression was of vast, still distance, endless reaches of sky, and uncounted flowers growing for their own pleasure and with no regard for human observation.

In studying Car Forty-seven, Katy was much impressed by the thoroughness of Mrs. Dayton's preparations for the comfort of her party. Everything that could possibly be needed seemed to have been thought of,—pins, cologne, sewing materials, all sorts of softening washes for the skin, to be used on the alkaline plains, sponges to wet and fasten into the crown of hats, other sponges to breathe through, medicines of various kinds, sticking-plaster, witch-hazel and arnica, whisk brooms, piles of magazines and novels, telegraph blanks, stationery. Nothing seemed forgotten. Clover said that it reminded her of the mother of the Swiss Family Robinson and that wonderful bag out of which everything was produced that could be thought of, from a grand piano to a bottle of pickles; and after that "Mrs. Robinson" became Mrs. Dayton's pet name among her fellow-travellers. She adopted it cheerfully; and her "wonderful bag" proving quite as unfailing and trustworthy as that of her prototype, the title seemed justified.

Pretty soon after starting came their first dinner on the car. Such a nice one!—soup, roast chicken and lamb, green peas, new potatoes, stewed tomato; all as hot and as perfectly served as if they had been "on dry land," as Amy phrased it. There was fresh curly lettuce too, with mayonnaise dressing, and a dessert of strawberries and ice-cream,—the latter made and frozen on the car, whose resources seemed inexhaustible. The cook had been attached to Car Forty-seven for some years, and had a celebrity on his own road for the preparation of certain dishes, which no one else could do as well, however many markets and refrigerators and kitchen ranges might be at command. One of these dishes was a peculiar form of cracked wheat, made crisp and savory after some mysterious fashion, and eaten with thick cream. Like most *chefs*, the cook liked to do the things in which he excelled, and finding that it was admired, he gave the party this delicious wheat every morning.

42

"The car seems paved with bottles of Apollinaris and with lemons," wrote Katy to her father. "There seems no limit to the supply. Just as surely as it grows warm and dusty, and we begin to remember that we are thirsty, a tinkle is heard, and Bayard appears with a tray,—iced lemonade, if you please, made with Apollinaris water with strawberries floating on top! What do you think of that at thirty miles an hour? Bayard is the colored butler. The cook is named Roland. We have a fine flavor of peers and paladins among us, you perceive.

"The first day out was cool and delicious, and we had no dust. At six o'clock we stopped at a junction, and our car was detached and run off on a siding. This was because Mr. Dayton had business in the place, and we were to wait and be taken on by the next express train soon after midnight. At first they ran us down to a pretty place by the side of the river, where it was cool, and we could look out on the water and a green bank opposite, and we thought we were going to have such a nice night; but the authorities changed their minds, and presently to our deep disgust a locomotive came puffing down the road, clawed us up, ran us back, and finally left us in the middle of innumerable tracks and switches just where all the freight trains came in and met. All night long they were arriving and going out. Cars loaded with cattle, cars loaded with sheep, with pigs! Such bleatings and mooings and gruntings, I never heard in all my life before. I could think of nothing but that verse in the Psalms, 'Strong bulls of Bashan have beset me round,' and could only hope that the poor animals did not feel half as badly as they sounded.

"Then long before light, as we lay listening to these lamentable roarings and grunts, and quite unable to sleep for heat and noise, came the blessed express, and presently we were away out of all the din, with the fresh air of the prairie blowing in; and in no time at all we were so sound asleep that it seemed but a minute before morning. Phil's slumbers lasted so long that we had to breakfast without him, for Mrs. Dayton would not let us wake him up. You can't think how kind she is, and Mr. Dayton too; and this way of travelling is so easy and delightful that it scarcely seems to tire one at all. Phil has borne the journey wonderfully well so far."

At Omaha, on the evening of the second day, Clover's future "matron" and adviser, Mrs. Watson, was to join them. She had been telegraphed to from Chicago, and had replied, so that they knew she was expecting them. Clover's thoughts were so occupied with curiosity as to what she would turn out to be, that she scarcely realized that she was crossing the Mississippi for the first time, and she gave scant attention to the low bluffs which bound the river, and on which the Indians used to hold their councils in those dim days when there was still an "undiscovered West" set down in geographies and atlases.

As soon as they reached the Omaha side of the river, she and Katy jumped down from the car, and immediately found themselves face to face with an anxious-looking little old lady, with white hair frizzled and banged over a puckered forehead, and a pair of watery blue eyes peering from beneath, evidently in search of somebody. Her hands were quite full of bags and parcels, and a little heap of similar articles lay on the platform near her, of which she seemed afraid to lose sight for a moment.

"Oh, is it Miss Carr?" was her first salutation. "I'm Mrs. Watson. I thought it might be you, from the fact that you got out of that car, and it seems rather different—I am quite relieved to see you. I didn't know but something—My daughter she said to me as I was coming away, 'Now, Mother, don't lose yourself, whatever you do. It seems quite wild to think of you in Canyon this and Canyon that, and the Garden of the Gods! Do get some one to keep an eye on you, or we shall never hear of you again. You'll—' It's quite a comfort that you have got here. I supposed you would, but the uncertainty—Oh, dear! that man is carrying off my trunks. Please run after him and tell him to bring them back!"

"It's all right; he's the porter," explained Mr. Dayton. "Did you get your checks for Denver or St. Helen's?"

"Oh, I haven't any checks yet. I didn't know which it ought to be, so I waited till—Miss Carr and her brother would see to it for me I knew, and I wrote my daughter—My friend, Mrs. Peters,—I've been staying with her, you know,—was sick in bed, and I wouldn't let—Dear me! what has that gentleman gone off for in such a hurry?"

"He has gone to get your checks," said Clover, divided between diversion and dismay at this specimen of her future "matron." "We only stay here a few minutes, I believe. Do you know exactly when the train starts, Mrs. Watson?"

"No, dear, I don't. I never know anything about trains and things like that. Somebody always has to tell me, and put me on the cars. I shall trust to you and your brother to do that now. It's a great comfort to have a gentleman to see to things for you."

A gentleman! Poor Philly!

Mr. Dayton now came back to them. It was lucky that he knew the station and was used to the ways of railroads, for it appeared that Mrs. Watson had made no arrangements whatever for her journey, but had blindly devolved the care of herself and her belongings on her "young friends," as she called Clover and Phil. She had no sleeping section secured and no tickets, and they had to be procured at the last moment and in such a scramble that the last of her parcels was handed on to the platform by a porter, at full run, after the train was in motion. She was not at all flurried by the commotion, though others were, and blandly repeated that she knew from the beginning that all would be right as soon as Miss Carr and her brother arrived.

Mrs. Dayton had sent a courteous invitation to the old lady to come to Car Forty-seven for tea, but Mrs. Watson did not at all like being left alone meantime, and held fast to Clover when the others moved to go.

"I'm used to being a good deal looked after," she explained. "All the family know my ways, and they never do let me be alone much. I'm taken faint sometimes; and the doctor says it's my heart or something that's the cause of it, so my daughter she—You ain't going, my dear, are you?"

"I must look after my brother," said poor Clover; "he's been ill, you know, and this is the time for his medicine."

"Dear me! is he ill?" said Mrs. Watson, in an aggrieved tone. "I wasn't prepared for that. You'll have your hands pretty full with him and me both, won't you?—for though I'm well enough just now, there's no knowing what a day may bring forth, and you're all I have to depend upon. You're sure you must go? It seems as if your sister—Mrs. Worthing, is that the name?—might see to the medicine, and give you a little freedom. Don't let your brother be too exacting, dear. It is the worst thing for a young man. I'll sit here a little while, and then I'll—The conductor will help me, I suppose, or perhaps that gentleman might—I hate to be left by myself."

These were the last words which Clover heard as she escaped. She entered Car Forty-seven with such a rueful and disgusted countenance that everybody burst out laughing.

"What is the matter, Miss Clover?" asked Mr. Dayton. "Has your old lady left something after all?"

"Don't call her *my* old lady! I'm supposed to be her young lady, under her charge," said Clover, trying to smile. But the moment she got Katy to herself, she burst out with,—

"My dear, what *am* I going to do? It's really too dreadful. Instead of some one to help me, which is what papa meant, Mrs. Watson seems to depend on me to take all the care of her; and she says she has fainting fits and disease of the heart! How can I take care of her? Phil needs me all the time, and a great deal more than she does; I don't see how I can."

"You can't, of course. You are here to take care of Phil; and it is out of the question that you should have another person to look after. But I think you must mistake Mrs. Watson, Clovy. I know that Mrs. Hall wrote plainly about Phil's illness, for she showed me the letter."

"Just wait till you hear her talk," cried the exasperated Clover. "You will find that I didn't mistake her at all. Oh, why did Mrs. Hall interfere? It would all seem so easy in comparison—so perfectly easy—if only Philly and I were alone together."

Katy thought that Clover was fretted and disposed to exaggerate; but after Mrs. Watson joined them a little later, she changed her opinion. The old lady was an inveterate talker, and her habit of only half finishing her sentences made it difficult to follow the meanderings of her rambling discourse. It turned largely on her daughter, Mrs. Phillips, her husband, children, house, furniture, habits, tastes, and the Phillips connection generally.

"She's the only one I've got," she informed Mrs. Dayton; "so of course she's all-important to me. Jane Phillips—that's Henry's youngest sister—often says that really of all the women she ever knew Ellen is the most—And there's plenty to do always, of course, with three children and such a large elegant house and company coming all the—It's lucky that there's plenty to do with. Henry's very liberal. He likes to have things nice, so Ellen she—Why, when I was packing up to come away he brought me that *repoussé* fruit-knife there in my bag—Oh, it's in my other bag! Never mind; I'll show it to you some other time—solid silver, you know. Bigelow and Kennard—their things always good, though expensive; and my son-in-law he said, 'You're going to a fruit country, and—' Mrs. Peters doesn't think there is so much fruit, though. All sent on from California, as I wrote,—and I guess Ellen and Henry were surprised to hear it."

Katy held serious counsel with herself that night as to what she should do about this extraordinary "guide, philosopher, and friend" whom the Fates had provided for Clover. She saw that her father, from very over-anxiety, had made a mistake, and complicated Clover's inevitable cares with a most undesirable companion, who would add to rather than relieve them. She could not decide what was best to do; and in fact the time was short for doing anything, for the next evening would bring them to Denver, and poor Clover must be left to face the situation by herself as best she might.

Katy finally concluded to write her father plainly how things stood, and beg him to set Clover's mind quite at rest as to any responsibility for Mrs. Watson, and also to have a talk with that lady herself, and explain matters as clearly as she could. It seemed all that was in her power.

Next day the party woke to a wonderful sense of lightness and exhilaration which no one could account for till the conductor told them that the apparently level plain over which they were speeding was more than four thousand feet above the sea. It seemed impossible to believe it. Hour by hour they climbed; but the climb was imperceptible. Now four thousand six hundred feet of elevation was reported, now four thousand eight hundred, at last above five thousand; and still there seemed about them nothing but a vast expanse of flat levels,—the table-lands of Nebraska. There was little that was beautiful in the landscape, which was principally made up of wide reaches of sand, dotted with cactus and grease-wood and with the droll cone-shaped burrows of the prairie-dogs, who could be seen gravely sitting on the roofs of their houses, or turning sudden somersaults in at the holes on top as the train whizzed by. They passed and repassed long links of a broad shallow river which the maps showed to be the Platte, and which seemed to be made of two-thirds sand to one-third water. Now and again mounted horsemen appeared in the distance whom Mr. Dayton said were "cow-boys;" but no cows were visible, and the rapidly moving figures were neither as picturesque nor as formidable as they had expected them to be.

Flowers were still abundant, and their splendid masses gave the charm of color to the rather arid landscape. Soon after noon dim blue outlines came into

view, which grew rapidly bolder and more distinct, and revealed themselves as the Rocky Mountains,—the "backbone of the American Continent," of which we have all heard so much in geographies and the newspapers. It was delightful, in spite of dust and glare, to sit with that sweep of magnificent air rushing into their lungs, and watch the great ranges grow and grow and deepen in hue, till they seemed close at hand. To Katy they were like enchanted land. Somewhere on the other side of them, on the dim Pacific coast, her husband was waiting for her to come, and the wheels seemed to revolve with a regular rhythmic beat to the cadence of the old Scotch song,—
"And will I see his face again;
And will I hear him speak?"

But to Clover the wheels sang something less jubilant, and she studied the mountains on her little travelling-map, and measured their distance from Burnet with a sigh. They were the walls of what seemed to her a sort of prison, as she realized that presently she should be left alone among them, Katy and Polly gone, and these new friends whom she had learned to like so much,—left alone with Phil and, what was worse, with Mrs. Watson! There was a comic side to the latter situation, undoubtedly, but at the moment she could not enjoy it.

Katy carried out her intention. She made a long call on Mrs. Watson in her section, and listened patiently to her bemoanings over the noise of the car which had kept her from sleeping; the "lady in gray over there" who had taken such a long time to dress in the morning that she—Mrs. Watson—could not get into the toilet-room at the precise moment that she wished; the newspaper boy who would not let her "just glance over" the Denver "Republican" unless she bought and paid for it ("and I only wanted to see the Washington news, my dear, and something about a tin wedding in East Dedham. My mother came from there, and I recognized one of the names and—But he took it away quite rudely; and when I complained, the conductor wouldn't attend to what I—"); and the bad piece of beefsteak which had been brought for her breakfast at the eating-station. Katy soothed and comforted to the best of her ability, and then plunged into her subject, explaining Phil's very delicate condition and the necessity for constant watchfulness on the part of Clover, and saying most distinctly and in the plainest of English that Mrs. Watson must not expect Clover to take care of her too. The old lady was not in the least offended; but her replies were so incoherent that Katy was not sure that she understood the matter any better for the explanation.

"Certainly, my dear, certainly. Your brother doesn't appear so very sick; but he must be looked after, of course. Boys always ought to be. I'll remind your sister if she seems to be forgetting anything. I hope I shall keep well myself, so as not to be a worry to her. And we can take little excursions together, I dare say—Girls always like to go, and of course an older person—Oh, no, your brother won't need her so much as you think. He seems pretty strong to me, and—You mustn't worry about them, Mrs. Worthing—We shall all get on very well, I'm sure, provided I don't break down, and I guess I sha'n't, though they say almost every one does in this air. Why, we shall be as high up as the top of Mount Washington."

Katy went back to Forty-seven in despair, to comfort herself with a long confidential chat with Clover in which she exhorted her not to let herself be imposed upon.

"Be good to her, and make her as happy as you can, but don't feel bound to wait on her, and run her errands. I am sure papa would not wish it; and it will half kill you if you attempt it. Phil, till he gets stronger, is all you can manage. You not only have to nurse him, you know, but to keep him happy. It's so bad for him to mope. You want all your time to read with him, and take walks and drives; that is, if there are any carriages at St. Helen's. Don't let Mrs. Watson seize upon you, Clover. I'm awfully afraid that she means to, and I can see that she is a real old woman of the sea. Once she gets on your back you will never be able to throw her off."

"She shall not get on my back," said Clover, straightening her small figure; "but doesn't it seem *unnecessary* that I should have an old woman of the sea to grapple with as well as Phil?"

"Provoking things are apt to seem unnecessary, I fancy. You mustn't let yourself get worried, dear Clovy. The old lady means kindly enough, I think, only she's naturally tiresome, and has become helpless from habit. Be nice to her, but hold your own. Self-preservation is the first law of Nature."

Just at dusk the train reached Denver, and the dreaded moment of parting came. There were kisses and tearful good-byes, but not much time was allowed for either. The last glimpse that Clover had of Katy was as the train moved away, when she put her head far out of the window of Car Forty-seven to kiss her hand once more, and call back, in a tone oracular and solemn enough to suit King Charles the First, his own admonitory word, "Remember!"

CHAPTER VI.

ST. HELEN'S.

Never in her life had Clover felt so small and incompetent and so very, very young as when the train with Car Forty-seven attached vanished from sight, and left her on the platform of the Denver station with her two companions. There they stood, Phil on one side tired and drooping, Mrs. Watson on the other blinking anxiously about, both evidently depending on her for guidance and direction. For one moment a sort of pale consternation swept over her. Then the sense of the inevitable and the nobler sense of responsibility came to her aid. She rallied herself; the color returned to her cheeks, and she said bravely to Mrs. Watson,—

"Now, if you and Phil will just sit down on that settee over there and make yourselves comfortable, I will find out about the trains for St. Helen's, and where we had better go for the night."

Mrs. Watson and Phil seated themselves accordingly, and Clover stood for a moment considering what she should do. Outside was a wilderness of tracks up and down which trains were puffing, in obedience, doubtless, to some law understood by themselves, but which looked to the uninitiated like the direst confusion. Inside the station the scene was equally confused. Travellers just arrived and just going away were rushing in and out; porters and baggage-agents with their hands full hurried to and fro. No one seemed at leisure to answer a question or even to listen to one.

Just then she caught sight of a shrewd, yet good-natured face looking at her from the window of the ticket-office; and without hesitation she went up to the enclosure. It was the ticket-agent whose eye she had caught. He was at liberty at the moment, and his answers to her inquiries, though brief, were polite and kind. People generally did soften to Clover. There was such an odd and pretty contrast between her girlish appealing look and her dignified little manner, like a child trying to be stately but only succeeding in being primly sweet.

The next train for St. Helen's left at nine in the morning, it seemed, and the ticket-agent recommended the Sherman House as a hotel where they would be very comfortable for the night.

"The omnibus is just outside," he said encouragingly. "You'll find it a first-class house,—best there is west of Chicago. From the East? Just so. You've not seen our opera-house yet, I suppose. Denver folks are rather proud of it. Biggest in the country except the new one in New York. Hope you'll find time to visit it."

"I should like to," said Clover; "but we are here for only one night. My brother's been ill, and we are going directly on to St. Helen's. I'm very much obliged to you."

Her look of pretty honest gratitude seemed to touch the heart of the ticket-man. He opened the door of his fastness, and came out—actually came out!— and with a long shrill whistle summoned a porter whom he addressed as, "Here, you Pat," and bade, "Take this lady's things, and put them into the 'bus for the Sherman; look sharp now, and see that she's all right." Then to Clover,—

"You'll find it very comfortable at the Sherman, Miss, and I hope you'll have a good night. If you'll come to me in the morning, I'll explain about the baggage transfer."

Clover thanked this obliging being again, and rejoined her party, who were patiently sitting where she had left them.

"Dear me!" said Mrs. Watson as the omnibus rolled off, "I had no idea that Denver was such a large place. Street cars too! Well, I declare!"

"And what nice shops!" said Clover, equally surprised.

Her ideas had been rather vague as to what was to be expected in the close neighborhood of the Rocky Mountains; but she knew that Denver had only existed a few years, and was prepared to find everything looking rough and unfinished.

"Why, they have restaurants here and jewellers' shops!" she cried. "Look, Phil, what a nice grocery! We needn't have packed all those oatmeal biscuits if only we had known. And electric lights! How wonderful! But of course St. Helen's is quite different."

Their amazement increased when they reached the hotel, and were taken in a large dining-room to order dinner from a bill of fare which seemed to include every known luxury, from Oregon salmon and Lake Superior white-fish to frozen sherbets and California peaches and apricots. But wonderment yielded to fatigue, and again as Clover fell asleep she was conscious of a deep depression. What had she undertaken to do? How could she do it?

But a night of sound sleep followed by such a morning of unclouded brilliance as is seldom seen east of Colorado banished these misgivings. Courage rose under the stimulus of such air and sunshine.

"I must just live for each day as it comes," said little Clover to herself, "do my best as things turn up, keep Phil happy, and satisfy Mrs. Watson,—if I can,—and not worry about to-morrows or yesterdays. That is the only safe way, and I won't forget if I can help it."

With these wise resolves she ran down stairs, looking so blithe and bright that Phil cheered at the sight of her, and lost the long morning face he had got up with, while even Mrs. Watson caught the contagion, and became fairly hopeful and content. A little leaven of good-will and good heart in one often avails to lighten the heaviness of many.

The distance between Denver and St. Helen's is less than a hundred miles, but as the railroad has to climb and cross a range of hills between two and three thousand feet high, the journey occupies several hours. As the train gradually rose higher and higher, the travellers began to get wide views, first of the magnificent panorama of mountains which lies to the northwest of Denver, sixty miles away, with Long's Peak in the middle, and after crossing the crest of the "Divide," where a blue little lake rimmed with wild-flowers sparkled in the sun, of the more southern ranges. After a while they found themselves running parallel to a mountain chain of strange and beautiful forms, green almost to the top, and intersected with deep ravines and cliffs which the conductor informed them were "canyons." They seemed quite near at hand, for their bases sank into low rounded hills covered with woods, these melted into undulating table-lands, and those again into a narrow strip of park-like plain across which ran the track. Flowers innumerable grew on this plain, mixed with grass of a tawny brown-green. There were cactuses, red and yellow, scarlet and white gillias, tall spikes of yucca in full bloom, and masses of a superb white poppy with an orange-brown centre, whose blue-green foliage was prickly like that of the thistle. Here and there on the higher uplands appeared strange rock shapes of red and pink and pale yellow, which looked like castles with towers and pinnacles, or like primitive fortifications. Clover thought it all strangely beautiful, but Mrs. Watson found fault with it as "queer."

"It looks unnatural, somehow," she objected; "not a bit like the East. Red never was a favorite color of mine. Ellen had a magenta bonnet once, and it always worried—But Henry liked it, so of course—People can't see things the same way. Now the green hat she had winter before last was—Don't you think those mountains are dreadfully bright and distinct? I don't like such high-colored rocks. Even the green looks red, somehow. I like soft, hazy mountains like Blue Hill and Wachusett. Ellen spent a summer up at Princeton once. It was when little Cynthia had diphtheria—she's named after me, you know, and Henry he thought—But I don't like the staring kind like these; and somehow those buildings, which the conductor says are not buildings but rocks, make my flesh creep."

"They'd be scrumptious places to repel attacks of Indians from," observed Phil; "two or three scouts with breech-loaders up on that scarlet wall there could keep off a hundred Piutes."

"I don't feel that way a bit," Clover was saying to Mrs. Watson. "I like the color, it's so rich; and I think the mountains are perfectly beautiful. If St. Helen's is like this I am going to like it, I know."

St. Helen's, when they reached it, proved to be very much "like this," only more so, as Phil remarked. The little settlement was built on a low plateau facing the mountains, and here the plain narrowed, and the beautiful range, seen through the clear atmosphere, seemed only a mile or two away, though in reality it was eight or ten. To the east the plain widened again into great upland sweeps like the Kentish Downs, with here and there a belt of black woodland, and here and there a line of low bluffs. Viewed from a height, with the cloud-shadows sweeping across it, it had the extent and splendor of the sea, and looked very much like it.

The town, seen from below, seemed a larger place than Clover had expected, and again she felt the creeping, nervous feeling come over her. But before the train had fairly stopped, a brisk, active little man jumped on board, and walking into the car, began to look about him with keen, observant eyes. After one sweeping glance, he came straight to where Clover was collecting her bags and parcels, held out his hand, and said in a pleasant voice, "I think this must be Miss Carr."

"I am Dr. Hope," he went on; "your father telegraphed when you were to leave Chicago, and I have come down to two or three trains in the hope of meeting you."

"Have you, indeed?" said Clover, with a rush of relief. "How very kind of you! And so papa telegraphed! I never thought of that. Phil, here is Dr. Hope, papa's friend; Dr. Hope, Mrs. Watson."

"This is really a very agreeable attention,—your coming to meet us," said Mrs. Watson; "a very agreeable attention indeed. Well, I shall write Ellen—that's my daughter, Mrs. Phillips, you know—that before we had got out of the cars, a gentleman—And though I've always been in the habit of going about a good deal, it's always been in the East, of course, and things are—What are we going to do first, Dr. Hope? Miss Carr has a great deal of energy for a girl, but naturally—I suppose there's an hotel at St. Helen's. Ellen is rather particular where I stay. 'At your age, Mother, you must be made comfortable, whatever it costs,' she says; and so I—An only daughter, you know—but you'll attend to all those things for us now, Doctor."

"There's quite a good hotel," said Dr. Hope, his eyes twinkling a little; "I'll show it to you as we drive up. You'll find it very comfortable if you prefer to go there. But for these young people I've taken rooms at a boarding-house, a quieter and less expensive place. I thought it was what your father would prefer," he added in a lower tone to Clover.

"I am sure he would," she replied; but Mrs. Watson broke in,—

"Oh, I shall go wherever Miss Carr goes. She's under my care, you know— Though at the same time I must say that in the long run I have generally found that the most expensive places turn out the cheapest. As Ellen often says, get the best and—What do they charge at this hotel that you speak of, Dr. Hope?"

"The Shoshone House? About twenty-five dollars a week, I think, if you make a permanent arrangement."

"That is a good deal," remarked Mrs. Watson, meditatively, while Clover hastened to say,—

"It is a great deal more than Phil and I can spend, Dr. Hope; I am glad you have chosen the other place for us."

"I suppose it is better," admitted Mm Watson; but when they gained the top of the hill, and a picturesque, many-gabled, many-balconied structure was pointed out as the Shoshone, her regrets returned, and she began again to murmur that very often the most expensive places turned out the cheapest in the end, and that it stood to reason that they must be the best. Dr. Hope rather encouraged this view, and proposed that she should stop and look at some rooms; but no, she could not desert her young charges and would go on, though at the same time she must say that her opinion as an older person who had seen more of the world was—She was used to being consulted. Why, Addy Phillips wouldn't order that crushed strawberry bengaline of hers till Mrs. Watson saw the sample, and—But girls had their own ideas, and were bound to carry them out, Ellen always said so, and for her part she knew her duty and meant to do it!

Dr. Hope flashed one rapid, comical look at Clover. Western life sharpens the wits, if it does nothing else, and Westerners as a general thing become pretty good judges of character. It had not taken ten minutes for the keen-witted little doctor to fathom the peculiarities of Clover's "chaperone," and he would most willingly have planted her in the congenial soil of the Shoshone House, which would have provided a wider field for her restlessness and self-occupation, and many more people to listen to her narratives and sympathize with her complaints. But it was no use. She was resolved to abide by the fortunes of her "young friends."

While this discussion was proceeding, the carriage had been rolling down a wide street running along the edge of the plateau, opposite the mountain range. Pretty houses stood on either side in green, shaded door-yards, with roses and vine-hung piazzas and nicely-cut grass.

"Why, it looks like a New England town," said Clover, amazed; "I thought there were no trees here."

"Yes, I know," said Dr. Hope smiling. "You came, like most Eastern people, prepared to find us sitting in the middle of a sandy waste, on cactus pincushions, picking our teeth with bowie-knives, and with no neighbors but Indians and grizzly bears. Well; sixteen years ago we could have filled the bill pretty well. Then there was not a single house in St. Helen's,—not even a tent, and not one of the trees that you see here had been planted. Now we have three railroads meeting at our depot, a population of nearly seven thousand, electric lights, telephones, a good opera-house, a system of works which brings first-rate spring water into the town from six miles away,—in short, pretty much all the modern conveniences."

"But what *has* made the place grow so fast?" asked Clover.

"If I may be allowed a professional pun, it is built up on coughings. It is a town for invalids. Half the people here came out for the benefit of their lungs."

"Isn't that rather depressing?"

"It would be more so if most of them did not look so well that no one would suspect them of being ill. Here we are."

Clover looked out eagerly. There was nothing picturesque about the house at whose gate the carriage had stopped. It was a large shabby structure, with a piazza above as well as below, and on these piazzas various people were sitting who looked unmistakably ill. The front of the house, however, commanded the fine mountain view.

"You see," explained Dr. Hope, drawing Clover aside, "boarding-places that are both comfortable and reasonable are rather scarce at St. Helen's. I know all about the table here and the drainage; and the view is desirable, and Mrs. Marsh, who keeps the house, is one of the best women we have. She's from down your way too,—Barnstable, Mass., I think."

Clover privately wondered how Barnstable, Mass., could be classed as "down" the same way with Burnet, not having learned as yet that to the soaring Western mind that insignificant fraction of the whole country known as "the East," means anywhere from Maine to Michigan, and that such trivial geographical differences as exist between the different sections seem scarcely worth consideration when compared with the vast spaces which lie beyond toward the setting sun. But perhaps Dr. Hope was only trying to tease her, for he twinkled amusedly at her puzzled face as he went on,—

"I think you can make yourselves comfortable here. It was the best I could do. But your old lady would be much better suited at the Shoshone, and I wish she'd go there."

Clover could not help laughing. "I wish that people wouldn't persist in calling Mrs. Watson my old lady," she thought.

Mrs. Marsh, a pleasant-looking person, came to meet them as they entered. She showed Clover and Phil their rooms, which had been secured for them, and then carried Mrs. Watson off to look at another which she could have if she liked.

The rooms were on the third floor. A big front one for Phil, with a sunny south window and two others looking towards the west and the mountains, and, opening from it, a smaller room for Clover.

"Your brother ought to live in fresh air both in doors and out," said Dr. Hope; "and I thought this large room would answer as a sort of sitting place for both of you."

"It's ever so nice; and we are both more obliged to you than we can say," replied Clover, holding out her hand as the doctor rose to go. He gave a pleased little laugh as he shook it.

"That's all right," he said. "I owe your father's children any good turn in my power, for he was a good friend to me when I was a poor boy just beginning, and needed friends. That's my house with the red roof, Miss Clover. You see how near it is; and please remember that besides the care of this boy here, I'm in charge of you too, and have the inside track of the rest of the friends you are going to make in Colorado. I expect to be called on whenever you want anything, or feel lonesome, or are at a loss in any way. My wife is coming to see you as soon as you have had your dinner and got settled a little. She sent those to you," indicating a vase on the table, filled with flowers. They were of a sort which Clover had never seen before,—deep cup-shaped blossoms of beautiful pale purple and white.

"Oh, what are they?" she called after the doctor.

"Anemones," he answered, and was gone.

"What a dear, nice, kind man!" cried Clover. "Isn't it delightful to have a friend right off who knows papa, and does things for us because we are papa's children? You like him, don't you, Phil; and don't you like your room?"

"Yes; only it doesn't seem fair that I should have the largest."

"Oh, yes; it is perfectly fair. I never shall want to be in mine except when I am dressing or asleep. I shall sit here with you all the time; and isn't it lovely that we have those enchanting mountains just before our eyes? I never saw anything in my life that I liked so much as I do that one."

It was Cheyenne Mountain at which she pointed, the last of the chain, and set a little apart, as it were, from the others. There is as much difference between mountains as between people, as mountain-lovers know, and like people they present characters and individualities of their own. The noble lines of Mount Cheyenne are full of a strange dignity; but it is dignity mixed with an indefinable charm. The canyons nestle about its base, as children at a parent's knee; its cedar forests clothe it like drapery; it lifts its head to the dawn and the sunset; and the sun seems to love it best of all, and lies longer on it than on the other peaks.

Clover did not analyze her impressions, but she fell in love with it at first sight, and loved it better and better all the time that she stayed at St. Helen's. "Dr. Hope and Mount Cheyenne were our first friends in the place," she used to say in after-days.

"How nice it is to be by ourselves!" said Phil, as he lay comfortably on the sofa watching Clover unpack. "I get so tired of being all the time with people. Dear me! the room looks quite homelike already."

Clover had spread a pretty towel over the bare table, laid some books and her writing-case upon it, and was now pinning up a photograph over the mantelpiece.

"We'll make it nice by-and-by," she said cheerfully; "and now that I've tidied up a little, I think I'll go and see what has become of Mrs. Watson. She'll think I have quite forgotten her. You'll lie quiet and rest till dinner, won't you?"

"Yes," said Phil, who looked very sleepy; "I'm all right for an hour to come. Don't hurry back if the ancient female wants you."

Clover spread a shawl over him before she went and shut one of the windows.

"We won't have you catching cold the very first morning," she said. "That would be a bad story to send back to papa."

She found Mrs. Watson in very low spirits about her room.

"It's not that it's small," she said. "I don't need a very big room; but I don't like being poked away at the back so. I've always had a front room all my life. And at Ellen's in the summer, I have a corner chamber, and see the sea and everything—It's an elegant room, solid black walnut with marble tops, and—Lighthouses too; I have three of them in view, and they are really company for me on dark nights. I don't want to be fussy, but really to look out on nothing but a side yard with some trees—and they aren't elms or anything that I'm used to, but a new kind. There's a thing out there, too, that I never saw before, which looks like one of the giant ants' nests of Africa in 'Morse's Geography' that I used to read about when I was—It makes me really nervous."

Clover went to the window to look at the mysterious object. It was a cone-shaped thing of white unburned clay, whose use she could not guess. She found later that it was a receptacle for ashes.

"I suppose *your* rooms are front ones?" went on Mrs. Watson, querulously.

"Mine isn't. It's quite a little one at the side. I think it must be just under this. Phil's is in front, and is a nice large one with a view of the mountains. I wish there were one just like it for you. The doctor says that it's very important for him to have a great deal of air in his room."

"Doctors always say that; and of course Dr. Hope, being a friend of yours and all—It's quite natural he should give you the preference. Though the Phillips's are accustomed—but there, it's no use; only, as I tell Ellen, Boston is the place for me, where my family is known, and people realize what I'm used to."

"I'm so sorry," Clover said again. "Perhaps somebody will go away, and Mrs. Marsh have a front room for you before long."

"She did say that she might. I suppose she thinks some of her boarders will be dying off. In fact, there is one—that tall man in gray in the reclining-chair—who didn't seem to me likely to last long. Well, we will hope for the best. I'm not one who likes to make difficulties."

This prospect, together with dinner, which was presently announced, raised Mrs. Watson's spirits a little, and Clover left her in the parlor, exchanging experiences and discussing symptoms with some ladies who had sat opposite them at table. Mrs. Hope came for a call; a pretty little woman, as friendly and kind as her husband. Then Clover and Phil went out for a stroll about the town. Their wonder increased at every turn; that a place so well equipped and complete in its appointments could have been created out of nothing in fifteen years was a marvel!

After two or three turns they found themselves among shops, whose plate-glass windows revealed all manner of wares,—confectionery, new books, pretty glass and china, bonnets of the latest fashion. One or two large pharmacies glittered with jars—purple and otherwise—enough to tempt any number of Rosamonds. Handsome carriages drawn by fine horses rolled past them, with well-dressed people inside. In short, St. Helen's was exactly like a thriving Eastern town of double its size, with the difference that here a great many more people seemed to ride than to drive. Some one cantered past every moment,—a lady alone, two or three girls together, or a party of rough-looking men in long boots, or a single ranchman sitting loose in his stirrups, and swinging a stock whip.

Clover and Phil were standing on a corner, looking at some "Rocky Mountain Curiosities" displayed for sale,—minerals, Pueblo pottery, stuffed animals, and Indian blankets; and Phil had just commented on the beauty of a black horse which was tied to a post close by, when its rider emerged from a shop, and prepared to mount.

He was a rather good-looking young fellow, sunburnt and not very tall, but with a lithe active figure, red-brown eyes and a long mustache of tawny chestnut. He wore spurs and a broad-brimmed sombrero, and carried in his hand a whip which seemed two-thirds lash. As he put his foot into the stirrup, he turned for another look at Clover, whom he had rather stared at while passing, and then changing his intention, took it out again, and came toward them.

"I beg your pardon," he said; "but aren't you—isn't it—Clover Carr?"

"Yes," said Clover, wondering, but still without the least notion as to whom the stranger might be.

"You've forgotten me?" went on the young man, with a smile which made his face very bright. "That's rather hard too; for I knew you at once. I suppose I'm a good deal changed, though, and perhaps I shouldn't have made you out except for your eyes; they're just the same. Why, Clover, I'm your cousin, Clarence Page!"

"Clarence Page!" cried Clover, joyfully; "not really! Why, Clarence, I never should have known you in the world, and I can't think how you came to know me. I was only fourteen when I saw you last, and you were quite a little boy. What good luck that we should meet, and on our first day too! Some one wrote that you were in Colorado, but I had no idea that you lived at St. Helen's."

"I don't; not much. I'm living on a ranch out that way," jerking his elbow toward the northwest, "but I ride in often to get the mail. Have you just come? You said the first day."

"Yes; we only got here this morning. And this is my brother Phil. Don't you recollect how I used to tell you about him at Ashburn?"

"I should think you did," shaking hands cordially; "she used to talk about you all the time, so that I felt intimately acquainted with all the family. Well, I call this first rate luck. It's two years since I saw any one from home."

"Home?"

"Well; the East, you know. It all seems like home when you're out here. And I mean any one that I know, of course. People from the East come out all the while. They are as thick as bumblebees at St. Helen's, but they don't amount to much unless you know them. Have you seen anything of mother and Lilly since they got back from Europe, Clover?"

"No, indeed. I haven't seen them since we left Hillsover. Katy has, though. She met them in Nice when she was there, and they sent her a wedding present. You knew that she was married, didn't you?"

"Yes, I got her cards. Pa sent them. He writes oftener than the others do; and he came out once and stayed a month on the ranch with me. That was while mother was in Europe. Where are you stopping? The Shoshone, I suppose."

"No, at a quieter place,—Mrs. Marsh's, on the same street."

"Oh, I know Mother Marsh. I went there when I first came out, and had caught the mountain fever, and she was ever so kind to me. I'm glad you are there. She's a nice woman."

"How far away is your ranch?"

"About sixteen miles. Oh, I say, Clover, you and Phil must come out and stay with us sometime this summer. We'll have a round-up for you if you will."

"What is a 'round-up' and who is 'us'?" said Clover, smiling.

"Well, a round-up is a kind of general muster of the stock. All the animals are driven in and counted, and the young ones branded. It's pretty exciting sometimes, I can tell you, for the cattle get wild, and it's all we can do to manage them. You should see some of our boys ride; it's splendid, and there's one half-breed that's the best hand with the lasso I ever saw. Phil will like it, I know. And 'us' is me and my partner."

"Have you a partner?"

"Yes, two, in fact; but one of them lives in New Mexico just now, so he does not count. That's Bert Talcott. He's a New York fellow. The other's English, a Devonshire man. Geoff Templestowe is his name."

"Is he nice?"

"You can just bet your pile that he is," said Clarence, who seemed to have assimilated Western slang with the rest of the West. "Wait till I bring him to see you. We'll come in on purpose some day soon. Well, I must be going. Good-by, Clover; good-by, Phil. It's awfully jolly to have you here."

"I never should have guessed who it was," remarked Clover, as they watched the active figure canter down the street and turn for a last flourish of the hat. "He was the roughest, scrubbiest boy when we last met. What a fine-looking fellow he has grown to be, and how well he rides!"

"No wonder; a fellow who can have a horse whenever he has a mind to," said Phil, enviously. "Life on a ranch must be great fun, I think."

"Yes; in one way, but pretty rough and lonely too, sometimes. It will be nice to go out and see Clarence's, if we can get some lady to go with us, won't it?"

"Well, just don't let it be Mrs. Watson, whoever else it is. She would spoil it all if she went."

"Now, Philly, don't. We're supposed to be leaning on her for support."

"Oh, come now, lean on that old thing! Why she couldn't support a postage stamp standing edgewise, as the man says in the play. Do you suppose I don't know how you have to look out for her and do everything? She's not a bit of use."

"Yes; but you and I have got to be polite to her, Philly. We mustn't forget that."

"Oh, I'll be polite enough, if she will just leave us alone," retorted Phil.

Promising!

CHAPTER VII.

MAKING ACQUAINTANCE.

Phil was better than his word. He was never uncivil to Mrs. Watson, and his distant manners, which really signified distaste, were set down by that lady to boyish shyness.

"They often are like that when they are young," she told Clover; "but they get bravely over it after a while. He'll outgrow it, dear, and you mustn't let it worry you a bit."

Meanwhile, Mrs. Watson's own flow of conversation was so ample that there was never any danger of awkward silences when she was present, which was a comfort. She had taken Clover into high favor now, and Clover deserved it,—for though she protected herself against encroachments, and resolutely kept the greater part of her time free for Phil, she was always considerate, and sweet in manner to the older lady, and she found spare half-hours every day in which to sit and go out with her, so that she should not feel neglected. Mrs. Watson grew quite fond of her "young friend," though she stood a little in awe of her too, and was disposed to be jealous if any one showed more attention to Clover than to herself.

An early outburst of this feeling came on the third day after their arrival, when Mrs. Hope asked Phil and Clover to dinner, and did *not* ask Mrs. Watson. She had discussed the point with her husband, but the doctor "jumped on" the idea forcibly, and protested that if that old thing was to come too, he would "have a consultation in Pueblo, and be off in the five thirty train, sure as fate."

"It's not that I care," Mrs. Watson assured Clover plaintively. "I've had so much done for me all my life that of course—But I *do* like to be properly treated. It isn't as if I were just anybody. I don't suppose Mrs. Hope knows much about Boston society anyway, but still—And I should think a girl from South Framingham (didn't you say she was from South Framingham?) would at least know who the Abraham Peabodys are, and they're Henry's—But I don't imagine she was much of anybody before she was married; and out here it's all hail fellow and well met, they say, though in that case I don't see—Well, well, it's no matter, only it seems queer to me; and I think you'd better drop a hint about it when you're there, and just explain that my daughter lives next door to the Lieutenant-Governor when she is in the country, and opposite the Assistant-Bishop in town, and has one of the Harvard Overseers for a near neighbor, and is distantly related to the Reveres! You'd think even a South Framingham girl must know about the lantern and the Old South, and how much they've always been respected at home."

Clover pacified her as well as she could, by assurances that it was not a dinner-party, and they were only asked to meet one girl whom Mrs. Hope wanted her to know.

"If it were a large affair, I am sure you would have been asked too," she said, and so left her "old woman of the sea" partly consoled.

It was the most lovely evening possible, as Clover and Phil walked down the street toward Dr. Hope's. Soft shadows lay over the lower spurs of the ranges. The canyons looked black and deep, but the peaks still glittered in rosy light. The mesa was in shadow, but the nearer plain lay in full sunshine, hot and yellow, and the west wind was full of mountain fragrance.

Phil gave little skips as he went along. Already he seemed like a different boy. All the droop and languor had gone, and given place to an exhilaration which half frightened Clover, who had constant trouble in keeping him from doing things which she knew to be imprudent. Dr. Hope had warned her that invalids often harmed themselves by over-exertion under the first stimulus of the high air.

"Why, how queer!" she exclaimed, stopping suddenly before one of the pretty places just above Mrs. Marsh's boarding-house.

"What?"

"Don't you see? That yard! When we came by here yesterday it was all green grass and rose-bushes, and girls were playing croquet; and now, look, it's a pond!"

Sure enough! There were the rose-bushes still, and the croquet arches; but they were standing, so to speak, up to their knees in pools of water, which seemed several inches deep, and covered the whole place, with the exception of the flagged walks which ran from the gates to the front and side doors of the house. Clover noticed now, for the first time, that these walks were several inches higher than the grass-beds on either side. She wondered if they were made so on purpose, and resolved to notice if the next place had the same arrangement.

But as they reached the next place and the next, lo! the phenomenon was repeated and Dr. Hope's lawn too was in the same condition,—everything was overlaid with water. They began to suspect what it must mean, and Mrs. Hope confirmed the suspicion. It was irrigation day in Mountain Avenue, it seemed. Every street in the town had its appointed period when the invaluable water, brought from a long distance for the purpose, was "laid on" and kept at a certain depth for a prescribed number of hours.

"We owe our grass and shrubs and flower-beds entirely to this arrangement," Mrs. Hope told them. "Nothing could live through our dry summers if we did not have the irrigating system."

"Are the summers so dry?" asked Clover. "It seems to me that we have had a thunder-storm almost every day since we came."

"We do have a good many thunderstorms," Mrs. Hope admitted; "but we can't depend on them for the gardens."

"And did you ever hear such magnificent thunder?" asked Dr. Hope. "Colorado thunder beats the world."

"Wait till you see our magnificent Colorado hail," put in Mrs. Hope, wickedly. "That beats the world, too. It cuts our flowers to pieces, and sometimes kills the sheep on the plains. We are very proud of it. The doctor thinks everything in Colorado perfection."

"I have always pitied places which had to be irrigated," remarked Clover, with her eyes fixed on the little twin-lakes which yesterday were lawns. "But I begin to think I was mistaken. It's very superior, of course, to have rains; but then at the East we sometimes don't have rain when we want it, and the grass gets dreadfully yellow. Don't you remember, Phil, how hard Katy and I worked last summer to keep the geraniums and fuschias alive in that long drought? Now, if we had had water like this to come once a week, and make a nice deep pond for us, how different it would have been!"

"Oh, you must come out West for real comfort," said Dr. Hope. "The East is a dreadfully one-horse little place, anyhow."

"But you don't mean New York and Boston when you say 'one-horse little place,' surely?"

"Don't I?" said the undaunted doctor. "Wait till you see more of us out here."

"Here's Poppy, at last," cried Mrs. Hope, as a girl came hurriedly up the walk. "You're late, dear."

"Poppy," whose real name was Marian Chase, was the girl who had been asked to meet them. She was a tall, rosy creature, to whom Clover took an instant fancy, and seemed in perfect health; yet she told them that when she came out to Colorado three years before, she had travelled on a mattress, with a doctor and a trained nurse in attendance.

"Your brother will be as strong, or stronger than I at the end of a year," she said; "or if he doesn't get well as fast as he ought, you must take him up to the Ute Valley. That's where I made my first gain."

"Where is the valley?"

"Thirty miles away to the northwest,—up there among the mountains. It is a great deal higher than this, and such a lovely peaceful place. I hope you'll go there."

"We shall, of course, if Phil needs it; but I like St. Helen's so much that I would rather stay here if we can."

Dinner was now announced, and Mrs. Hope led the way into a pretty room hung with engravings and old plates after the modern fashion, where a white-spread table stood decorated with wild-flowers, candle-sticks with little red-shaded tapers, and a pyramid of plums and apricots. There was the usual succession of soup and fish and roast and salad which one looks for at a dinner on the sea-level, winding up with ice-cream of a highly civilized description, but Clover could scarcely eat for wondering how all these things had come there so soon, so very soon. It seemed like magic,—one minute the solemn peaks and passes, the prairie-dogs and the thorny plain, the next all these portières and rugs and etchings and down pillows and pretty devices in glass and china, as if some enchanter's wand had tapped the wilderness, and, hey, presto! modern civilization had sprung up like Jonah's gourd all in a minute, or like the palace which Aladdin summoned into being in a single night for the occupation of the Princess of China, by the rubbing of his wonderful lamp. And then, just as the fruit-plates were put on the table, came a call, and the doctor was out in the hall, "holloing" and conducting with some distant patient one of those mysterious telephonic conversations which to those who overhear seem all replies and no questions. It was most remarkable, and quite unlike her preconceived ideas of what was likely to take place at the base of the Rocky Mountains.

A pleasant evening followed. "Poppy" played delightfully on the piano; later came a rubber of whist. It was like home.

"Before these children go, let us settle about the drive," said Dr. Hope to his wife.

"Oh, yes! Miss Carr—"

"Oh, please, won't you call me Clover?"

"Indeed I will,—Clover, then,—we want to take you for a good long drive to-morrow, and show you something; but the trouble is, the doctor and I are at variance as to what the something shall be. I want you to see Odin's Garden; and the doctor insists that you ought to go to the Cheyenne canyons first, because those are his favorites. Now, which shall it be? We will leave it to you."

"But how can I choose? I don't know either of them. What a queer name,— Odin's Garden!"

"I'll tell you how to settle it," cried Marian Chase, whose nickname it seemed had been given her because when she first came to St. Helen's she wore a bunch of poppies in her hat. "Take them to Cheyenne to-morrow; and the next day— or Thursday—let me get up a picnic for Odin's Garden; just a few of our special cronies,—the Allans and the Blanchards and Mary Pelham and Will Amory. Will you, dear Mrs. Hope, and be our matron? That would be lovely."

Mrs. Hope consented, and Clover walked home as if treading on air. Was this the St. Helen's to which she had looked forward with so much dread,—this gay, delightful place, where such pleasant things happened, and people were so kind? How she wished that she could get at Katy and papa for five minutes—on a wishing carpet or something—to tell them how different everything was from what she had expected.

One thing only marred her anticipations for the morrow, which was the fear that Mrs. Watson might be hurt, and make a scene. Happily, Mrs. Hope's thoughts took the same direction; and by some occult process of influence, the use of which good wives understand, she prevailed on her refractory doctor to allow the old lady to be asked to join the party.

So early next morning came a very polite note; and it was proposed that Phil should ride the doctor's horse, and act as escort to Miss Chase, who was to go on horseback likewise. No proposal could have been more agreeable to Phil, who adored horses, and seldom had the chance to mount one; so every one was pleased, and Mrs. Watson preened her ancestral feathers with great satisfaction.

"You see, dear, how well it was to give that little hint about the Reveres and the Abraham Peabodys," she said. Clover felt dreadfully dishonest; but she dared not confess that she had forgotten all about the hint, still less that she had never meant to give one. "The better part of valor is discretion," she remembered; so she held her peace, though her cheeks glowed guiltily.

At three o'clock they set forth in a light roomy carriage,—not exactly a carryall, but of the carryall family,—with a pair of fast horses, Miss Chase and Phil cantering happily alongside, or before or behind, just as it happened. The sun was very hot; but there was a delicious breeze, and the dryness and elasticity of the air made the heat easy to bear.

The way lay across and down the southern slope of the plateau on which the town was built. Then they came to splendid fields of grain and "afalfa,"—a cereal quite new to them, with broad, very green leaves. The roadside was gay with flowers,—gillias and mountain balm; high pink and purple spikes, like foxgloves, which they were told were pentstemons; painters' brush, whose green tips seemed dipped in liquid vermilion, and masses of the splendid wild poppies. They crossed a foaming little river; and a sharp turn brought them into a narrower and wilder road, which ran straight toward the mountain side. This was overhung by trees, whose shade was grateful after the hot sun.

Narrower and narrower grew the road, more and more sharp the turns. They were at the entrance of a deep defile, up which the road wound and wound, following the links of the river, which they crossed and recrossed repeatedly. Such a wonderful and perfect little river, with water clear as air and cold as ice, flowing over a bed of smooth granite, here slipping noiselessly down long slopes of rock like thin films of glass, there deepening into pools of translucent blue-green like aqua-marine or beryl, again plunging down in mimic waterfalls, a sheet of iridescent foam. The sound of its rush and its ripple was like a laugh. Never was such happy water, Clover thought, as it curved and bent and swayed this way and that on its downward course as if moved by some merry, capricious instinct, like a child dancing as it goes. Regiments or great ferns grew along its banks, and immense thickets of wild roses of all shades, from deep Jacqueminot red to pale blush-white. Here and there rose a lonely spike of yucca, and in the little ravines to right and left grew in the crevices of the rocks clumps of superb straw-colored columbines four feet high.

Looking up, Clover saw above the tree-tops strange pinnacles and spires and obelisks which seemed air-hung, of purple-red and orange-tawny and pale pinkish gray and terra cotta, in which the sunshine and the cloud-shadows broke in a multiplicity of wonderful half-tints. Above them was the dazzling blue of the Colorado sky. She drew a long, long breath.

"So this is a canyon," she said. "How glad I am that I have lived to see one."

"Yes, this is a canyon," Dr. Hope replied. "Some of us think it *the* canyon; but there are dozens of others, and no two of them are alike. I'm glad you are pleased with this, for it's my favorite. I wish your father could see it."

Clover hardly understood what he said she was so fascinated and absorbed. She looked up at the bright pinnacles, down at the flowers and the sheen of the river-pools and the mad rush of its cascades, and felt as though she were in a dream. Through the dream she caught half-comprehended fragments of conversation from the seat behind. Mrs. Watson was giving her impressions of the scenery.

"It's pretty, I suppose," she remarked; "but it's so very queer, and I'm not used to queer things. And this road is frightfully narrow. If a load of hay or a big Concord coach should come along, I can't think what we should do. I see that Dr. Hope drives carefully, but yet—You don't think we shall meet anything of the kind to-day, do you, Doctor?"

"Not a Concord coach, and certainly not a hay-wagon, for they don't make hay up here in the mountains."

"Well, that is a relief. I didn't know. Ellen she always says, 'Mother, you're a real fidget;' but when one grows old, and has valves in the heart as I have, you never—We might meet one of those big pedler's wagons, though, and they frighten horses worse than anything. Oh, what's that coming now? Let us get out, Dr. Hope; pray, let us all get out."

"Sit still, ma'am," said the doctor, sternly, for Mrs. Watson was wildly fumbling at the fastening of the door. "Mary, put your arm round Mrs. Watson, and hold her tight. There'll be a real accident, sure as fate, if you don't." Then in a gentler tone, "It's only a buggy, ma'am; there's plenty of room. There's no possible risk of a pedler's wagon. What on earth should a pedler be doing up here on the side of Cheyenne! Prairie-dogs don't use pomatum or tin-ware."

"Oh, I didn't know," repeated poor Mrs. Watson, nervously. She watched the buggy timorously till it was safely past; then her spirits revived.

"Well," she cried, "we're safe this time; but I call it tempting Providence to drive so fast on such a rough road. If all canyons are as wild as this, I sha'n't ever venture to go into another."

"Bless me! this is one of our mildest specimens," said Dr. Hope, who seemed to have a perverse desire to give Mrs. Watson a distaste for canyons. "This is a smooth one; but some canyons are really rough. Do you remember, Mary, the day we got stuck up at the top of the Westmoreland, and had to unhitch the horses, and how I stood in the middle of the creek and yanked the carriage round while you held them? That was the day we heard the mountain lion, and there were fresh bear-tracks all over the mud, you remember."

"Good gracious!" cried Mrs. Watson, quite pale; "what an awful place! Bears and lions! What on earth did you go there for?"

"Oh, purely for pleasure," replied the doctor, lightly. "We don't mind such little matters out West. We try to accustom ourselves to wild beasts, and make friends of them."

"John, don't talk such nonsense," cried his wife, quite angrily. "Mrs. Watson, you mustn't believe a word the doctor says. I've lived in Colorado nine years; and I've never once seen a mountain lion, or a bear either, except the stuffed ones in the shops. Don't let the doctor frighten you."

But Dr. Hope's wicked work was done. Mrs. Watson, quite unconvinced by these well-meant assurances, sat pale and awe-struck, repeating under her breath,—

"Dreadful! What *will* Ellen say? Bears and lions! Oh, dear me!"

"Look, look!" cried Clover, who had not listened to a word of this conversation; "did you ever see anything so lovely?" She referred to what she was looking at,—a small point of pale straw-colored rock some hundreds of feet in height, which a turn in the road had just revealed, soaring above the tops of the trees.

"I don't see that it's lovely at all," said Mrs. Watson, testily. "It's unnatural, if that's what you mean. Rocks ought not to be that color. They never are at the East. It looks to me exactly like an enormous unripe banana standing on end."

This simile nearly "finished" the party. "It's big enough to disagree with all the Sunday-schools in creation at once," remarked the doctor, between his shouts, while even Clover shook with laughter. Mrs. Watson felt that she had made a hit, and grew complacent again.

"See what your brother picked for me," cried Poppy, riding alongside, and exhibiting a great sheaf of columbine tied to the pommel of her saddle. "And how do you like North Cheyenne? Isn't it an exquisite place?"

"Perfectly lovely; I feel as if I must come here every day."

"Yes, I know; but there are so many other places out here about which you have that feeling."

"Now we will show you the other Cheyenne Canyon,—the twin of this," said Dr. Hope; "but you must prepare your mind to find it entirely different."

After rather a rough mile or two through woods, they came to a wooden shed, or shanty, at the mouth of a gorge, and here Dr. Hope drew up his horses, and helped them all out.

"Is it much of a walk?" asked Mrs. Watson.

"It is rather long and rather steep," said Mrs. Hope; "but it is lovely if you only go a little way in, and you and I will sit down the moment you feel tired, and let the others go forward."

South Cheyenne Canyon was indeed "entirely different." Instead of a green-floored, vine-hung ravine, it is a wild mountain gorge, walled with precipitous cliffs of great height; and its river—every canyon has a river—comes from a source at the top of the gorge in a series of mad leaps, forming seven waterfalls, which plunge into circular basins of rock, worn smooth by the action of the stream. These pools are curiously various in shape, and the color of the water, as it pauses a moment to rest in each before taking its next plunge, is beautiful. Little plank walks are laid along the river-side, and rude staircases for the steepest pitches. Up these the party went, leaving Mrs. Watson and Mrs. Hope far behind,—Poppy with her habit over her arm, Clover stopping every other moment to pick some new flower, Phil shying stones into the rapids as he passed,—till the top of the topmost cascade was reached, and looking back they could see the whole wonderful way by which they had climbed, and down which the river made its turbulent rush. Clover gathered a great mat of green scarlet-berried vine like glorified cranberry, which Dr. Hope told her was the famous kinnikinnick, and was just remarking on the cool water-sounds which filled the place, when all of a sudden these sounds seemed to grow angry, the defile of precipices turned a frowning blue, and looking up they saw a great thunder-cloud gathering overhead.

"We must run," cried Dr. Hope, and down they flew, racing at full speed along the long flights of steps and the plank walks, which echoed to the sound of their flying feet. Far below they could see two fast-moving specks which they guessed to be Mrs. Hope and Mrs. Watson, hurrying to a place of shelter. Nearer and nearer came the storm, louder the growl of the thunder, and great hail-stones pattered on their heads before they gained the cabin; none too soon, for in another moment the cloud broke, and the air was full of a dizzy whirl of sleet and rain.

Others besides themselves had been surprised in the ravine, and every few minutes another and another wet figure would come flying down the path, so that the little refuge was soon full. The storm lasted half an hour, then it scattered as rapidly as it had come, the sun broke out brilliantly, and the drive home would have been delightful if it had not been for the sad fact that Mrs. Watson had left her parasol in the carriage, and it had been wet, and somewhat stained by the india-rubber blanket which had been thrown over it for protection. Her lamentations were pathetic.

"Jane Phillips gave it to me,—she was a Sampson, you know,—and I thought ever so much of it. It was at Hovey's—We were there together, and I admired it; and she said, 'Mrs. Watson, you must let me—' Six dollars was the price of it. That's a good deal for a parasol, you know, unless it's really a nice one; but Hovey's things are always—I had the handle shortened a little just before I came away, too, so that it would go into my trunk; it had to be mended anyhow, so that it seemed a good—Dear, dear! and now it's spoiled! What a pity I left it in the carriage! I shall know better another time, but this climate is so different. It never rains in this way at home. It takes a little while about it, and gives notice; and we say that there's going to be a northeaster, or that it looks like a thunder-storm, and we put on our second-best clothes or we stay at home. It's a great deal nicer, I think."

"I am so sorry," said kind little Mrs. Hope. "Our storms out here do come up very suddenly. I wish I had noticed that you had left your parasol. Well, Clover, you've had a chance now to see the doctor's beautiful Colorado hail and thunder to perfection. How do you like them?"

"I like everything in Colorado, I believe," replied Clover, laughing. "I won't even except the hail."

"She's the girl for this part of the world," cried Dr. Hope, approvingly. "She'd make a first-rate pioneer. We'll keep her out here, Mary, and never let her go home. She was born to live at the West."

"Was I? It seems queer then that I should have been born to live in Burnet."

"Oh, we'll change all that."

"I'm sure I don't see how."

"There are ways and means," oracularly.

Mrs. Watson was so cast down by the misadventure to her parasol that she expressed no regret at not being asked to join in the picnic next day, especially as she understood that it consisted of young people. Mrs. Hope very rightly decided that a whole day out of doors, in a rough place, would give pain rather than pleasure to a person who was both so feeble and so fussy, and did not suggest her going. Clover and Phil waked up quite fresh and untired after a sound night's sleep. There seemed no limit to what might be done and enjoyed in that inexhaustibly renovating air.

Odin's Garden proved to be a wonderful assemblage of rocky shapes rising from the grass and flowers of a lonely little plain on the far side of the mesa, four or five miles from St. Helen's. The name of the place came probably from something suggestive in the forms of the rocks, which reminded Clover of pictures she had seen of Assyrian and Egyptian rock carvings. There were lion shapes and bull shapes like the rudely chiselled gods of some heathen worship; there were slender, points and obelisks three hundred feet high; and something suggesting a cat-faced deity, and queer similitudes of crocodiles and apes,—all in the strange orange and red and pale yellow formations of the region. It was a wonderful rather than a beautiful place; but the day was spent very happily under those mysterious stones, which, as the long afternoon shadows gathered over the plain, and the sky glowed with sunset crimson which seemed like a reflection from the rocks themselves, became more mysterious still. Of the merry young party which made up the picnic, seven out of nine had come to Colorado for health; but no one would have guessed it, they seemed so well and so full of the enjoyment of life. Altogether, it was a day to be marked; not with a white stone,—that would not have seemed appropriate to Colorado,—but with a red one. Clover, writing about it afterward to Elsie, felt that her descriptions to sober stay-at-homes might easily sound overdrawn and exaggerated, and wound up her letter thus:—

"Perhaps you think that I am romancing; but I am not a bit.
Every word I say is perfectly true, only I have not made the
colors half bright or the things half beautiful enough. Colorado
is the most beautiful place in the world. [N.B.—Clover had seen
but a limited portion of the world so far.] I only wish you
could all come out to observe for yourselves that I am not
fibbing, though it sounds like it!"

CHAPTER VIII.

HIGH VALLEY.

Clover was putting Phil's chamber to rights, and turning it into a sitting-room for the day, which was always her first task in the morning. They had been at St. Helen's nearly three weeks now, and the place had taken on a very homelike appearance. All the books and the photographs were unpacked, the washstand had vanished behind a screen made of a three-leaved clothes-frame draped with chintz, while a ruffled cover of the same gay chintz, on which bunches of crimson and pink geraniums straggled over a cream-colored ground, gave to the narrow bed the air of a respectable wide sofa.

"There! those look very nice, I think," she said, giving the last touch to a bowl full of beautiful garden roses. "How sweet they are!"

"Your young man seems rather clever about roses," remarked Phil, who, boy-like, dearly loved to tease his sister.

"My young man, as you call him, has a father with a gardener," replied Clover, calmly; "no very brilliant cleverness is required for that."

In a cordial, kindly place, like St. Helen's, people soon make acquaintances, and Clover and Phil felt as if they already knew half the people in the town. Every one had come to see them and deluged them with flowers, and invitations to dine, to drive, to take tea. Among the rest came Mr. Thurber Wade, whom Phil was pleased to call Clover's young man,—the son of a rich New York banker, whose ill-health had brought him to live in St. Helen's, and who had built a handsome house on the principal street. This gilded youth had several times sent roses to Clover,—a fact which Phil had noticed, and upon which he was fond of commenting.

"Speaking of young men," went on Clover, "what do you suppose has become of Clarence Page? He said he should come in to see us soon; but that was ever so long ago."

"He's a fraud, I suspect," replied Phil, lazily, from his seat in the window. He had a geometry on his knees, and was supposed to be going on with his education, but in reality he was looking at the mountains. "I suppose people are pretty busy on ranches, though," he added. "Perhaps they're sheep-shearing."

"Oh, it isn't a sheep ranch. Don't you remember his saying that the cattle got very wild, and they had to ride after them? They wouldn't ride after sheep. I hope he hasn't forgotten about us. I was so glad to see him."

While this talk went on, Clarence was cantering down the lower end of the Ute Pass on his way to St. Helen's. Three hours later his name was brought up to them.

"How nice!" cried Clover. "I think as he's a relative we might let him come here, Phil. It's so much pleasanter than the parlor."

Clarence, who had passed the interval of waiting in noting the different varieties of cough among the sick people in the parlor, was quite of her opinion.

"How jolly you look!" was almost his first remark. "I'm glad you've got a little place of your own, and don't have to sit with those poor creatures downstairs all the time."

"It is much nicer. Some of them are getting better, though."

"Some of them aren't. There's one poor fellow in a reclining-chair who looks badly."

"That's the one whose room Mrs. Watson has marked for her own. She asks him three times a day how he feels, with all the solicitude of a mother," said Phil.

"Who's Mrs. Watson?"

"Well, she's an old lady who is somehow fastened to us, and who considers herself our chaperone," replied Clover, with a little laugh. "I must introduce you by-and-by, but first we want a good talk all by ourselves. Now tell us why you haven't come to see us before. We have been hoping for you every day."

"Well, I've wanted to come badly enough, but there has been a combination of hindrances. Two of our men got sick, so there was more to do than usual; then Geoff had to be away four days, and almost as soon as he got back he had bad news from home, and I hated to leave him alone."

"What sort of bad news?"

"His sister's dead."

"Poor fellow! In England too! You said he was English, didn't you?"

"Yes. She was married. Her husband was a clergyman down in Cornwall somewhere. She was older than Geoff a good deal; but he was very fond of her, and the news cut him up dreadfully."

"No wonder. It is horrible to hear such a thing when one is far from home," observed Clover. She tried to realize how she should feel if word came to St. Helen's of Katy's death, or Elsie's, or Johnnie's; but her mind refused to accept the question. The very idea made her shiver.

"Poor fellow!" she said again; "what could you do for him, Clarence?"

"Not much. I'm a poor hand at comforting any one,—men generally are, I guess. Geoff knows I'm sorry for him; but it takes a woman to say the right thing at such times. We sit and smoke when the work's done, and I know what he's thinking about; but we don't say anything to each other. Now let's speak of something else. I want to settle about your coming to High Valley."

"High Valley? Is that the name of your place?"

"Yes. I want you to see it. It's an awfully pretty place to my thinking,—not so very much higher than this, but you have to climb a good deal to get there. Can't you come? This is just the time,—raspberries ripe, and lots of flowers wherever the beasts don't get at them. Phil can have all the riding he wants, and it'll do poor Geoff lots of good to see some one."

"It would be very nice indeed," doubtfully; "but who could we get to go with us?"

"I thought of that. We don't take much stock in Mrs. Grundy out here; but I supposed you'd want another lady. How would it be if I asked Mrs. Hope? The doctor's got to come out anyway to see one of our herders who's put his shoulder out in a fall. If he would drive you out, and Mrs. Hope would stay on, would you come for a week? I guess you'll like it."

"I 'guess' we should," exclaimed Clover, her face lighting up. "Clarence, how delightful it sounds! It will be lovely to come if Mrs. Hope says yes."

"Then that's all right," replied Clarence, looking extremely pleased. "I'll ride up to the doctor's as soon as dinner's over."

"You'll dine with us, of course?"

"Oh, I always come to Mother Marsh for a bite whenever I stay over the day. She likes to have me. We've been great chums ever since I had fever here, and she took care of me."

Clover was amused at dinner to watch the cool deliberation with which Clarence studied Mrs. Watson and her tortuous conversation, and, as he would have expressed it, "took stock of her." The result was not favorable, apparently.

"What on earth did they send that old thing with you for?" he asked as soon as they went upstairs. "She's as much out of her element here as a canary-bird would be in a cyclone. She can't be any use to you, Clover."

"Well, no; I don't think she is. It was a sort of mistake; I'll tell you about it sometime. But she likes to imagine that she's taking care of me; and as it does no harm, I let her."

"Taking care of you! Great thunder! I wouldn't trust her to take care of a blue-eyed kitten," observed the irreverent Clarence. "Well, I'll ride up and settle with the Hopes, and stop and let you know as I come back."

Mrs. Hope and the doctor were not hard to persuade. In Colorado, people keep their lamps of enjoyment filled and trimmed, so to speak, and their travelling energies ready girt about them, and easily adopt any plan which promises pleasure. The following day was fixed for the start, and Clover packed her valise and Phil's bag, with a sense of exhilaration and escape. She was, in truth, getting very tired of the exactions of Mrs. Watson. Mrs. Watson, on her part, did not at all approve of the excursion.

"I think," she said, swelling with offended dignity, "that your cousin didn't know much about politeness when he left me out of his invitation and asked Mrs. Hope instead. Yes, I know; the doctor had to go up anyway. That may be true, and it may not; but it doesn't alter the case. What am I to do, I should like to know, if the valves of my heart don't open, or don't shut—whichever it is—while I'm left all alone here among strangers?"

"Send for Dr. Hope," suggested Phil. "He'll only be gone one night. Clover doesn't know anything about valves."

"My cousin lives in a rather rough way, I imagine," interposed Clover, with a reproving look at Phil. "He would hardly like to ask a stranger and an invalid to his house, when he might not be able to make her comfortable. Mrs. Hope has been there before, and she's an old friend."

"Oh, I dare say! There are always reasons. I don't say that I should have felt like going, but he ought to have asked me. Ellen will be surprised, and so will—He's from Ashburn too, and he must know the Parmenters, and Mrs. Parmenter's brother's son is partner to Henry's brother-in-law. It's of no consequence, of course,—still, respect—older people—Boston—not used to—Phillips—" Mrs. Watson's voice died away into fragmentary and inaudible lamentings.

Clover attempted no further excuse. Her good sense told her that she had a perfect right to accept this little pleasure; that Mrs. Watson's plans for Western travel had been formed quite independently of their own, and that papa would not wish her to sacrifice herself and Phil to such unreasonable humors. Still, it was not pleasant; and I am sorry to say that from this time dated a change of feeling on Mrs. Watson's part toward her "young friends." She took up a chronic position of grievance toward them, confided her wrongs to all new-comers, and met Clover with an offended air which, though Clover ignored it, did not add to the happiness of her life at Mrs. Marsh's.

It was early in the afternoon when they started, and the sun was just dipping behind the mountain wall when they drove into the High Valley. It was one of those natural parks, four miles long, which lie like heaven-planted gardens among the Colorado ranges. The richest of grass clothed it; fine trees grew in clumps and clusters here and there; and the spaces about the house where fences of barbed wire defended the grass from the cattle, seemed a carpet of wild-flowers.

Clover exclaimed with delight at the view. The ranges which lapped and held the high, sheltered upland in embrace opened toward the south, and revealed a splendid lonely peak, on whose summit a drift of freshly-fallen snow was lying. The contrast with the verdure and bloom below was charming.

The cabin—it was little more—stood facing this view, and was backed by a group of noble red cedars. It was built of logs, long and low, with a rude porch in front supported on unbarked tree trunks. Two fine collies rushed to meet them, barking vociferously; and at the sound Clarence hurried to the door. He met them with great enthusiasm, lifted out Mrs. Hope, then Clover, and then began shouting for his chum, who was inside.

"Hollo, Geoff! where are you? Hurry up; they've come." Then, as he appeared, "Ladies and gentleman, my partner!"

Geoffrey Templestowe was a tall, sinewy young Englishman, with ruddy hair and beard, grave blue eyes, and an unmistakable air of good breeding. He wore a blue flannel shirt and high boots like Clarence's, yet somehow he made Clarence look a little rough and undistinguished. He was quiet in speech, reserved in manner, and seemed depressed and under a cloud; but Clover liked his face at once. He looked both strong and kind, she thought.

The house consisted of one large square room in the middle, which served as parlor and dining-room both, and on either side two bedrooms. The kitchen was in a separate building. There was no lack of comfort, though things were rather rude, and the place had a bare, masculine look. The floor was strewn with coyote and fox skins. Two or three easy-chairs stood around the fireplace, in which, July as it was, a big log was blazing. Their covers were shabby and worn; but they looked comfortable, and were evidently in constant use. There was not the least attempt at prettiness anywhere. Pipes and books and old newspapers littered the chairs and tables; when an extra seat was needed Clarence simply tipped a great pile of these on to the floor. A gun-rack hung upon the wall, together with sundry long stock-whips and two or three pairs of spurs, and a smell of tobacco pervaded the place.

Clover's eyes wandered to a corner where stood a small parlor organ, and over it a shelf of books. She rose to examine them. To her surprise they were all hymnals and Church of England prayer-books. There were no others. She wondered what it meant.

Clarence had given up his own bedroom to Phil, and was to chum with his friend. Some little attempt had been made to adorn the rooms which were meant for the ladies. Clean towels had been spread over the pine shelves which did duty for dressing-tables, and on each stood a tumbler stuffed as full as it could hold with purple pentstemons. Clover could not help laughing, yet there was something pathetic to her in the clumsy, man-like arrangement. She relieved the tumbler by putting a few of the flowers in her dress, and went out again to the parlor, where Mrs. Hope sat by the fire, quizzing the two partners, who were hard at work setting their tea-table.

It was rather a droll spectacle,—the two muscular young fellows creaking to and fro in their heavy boots, and taking such an infinitude of pains with their operations. One would set a plate on the table, and the other would forthwith alter its position slightly, or lift and scrutinize a tumbler and dust it sedulously with a glass-towel. Each spoon was polished with the greatest particularity before it was laid on the tray; each knife passed under inspection. Visitors were not an every-day luxury in the High Valley, and too much care could not be taken for their entertainment, it seemed.

Supper was brought in by a Chinese cook in a pigtail, wooden shoes, and a blue Mother Hubbard, Choo Loo by name. He was evidently a good cook, for the corn-bread and fresh mountain trout and the ham and eggs were savory to the last degree, and the flapjacks, with which the meal concluded, and which were eaten with a sauce of melted raspberry jelly, deserved even higher encomium.

"We are willing to be treated as company this first night," observed Mrs. Hope; "but if you are going to keep us a week, you must let us make ourselves useful, and set the table and arrange the rooms for you."

"We will begin to-morrow morning," added Clover. "May we, Clarence? May we play that it is our house, and do what we like, and change about and arrange things? It will be such fun."

"Fire away!" said her cousin, calmly. "The more you change the more we shall like it. Geoff and I aren't set in our ways, and are glad enough to be let off duty for a week. The hut is yours just as long as you will stay; do just what you like with it. Though we're pretty good housekeepers too, considering; don't you think so?"

"Do you believe he meant it?" asked Clover, confidentially afterward of Mrs. Hope. "Do you think they really wouldn't mind being tidied up a little? I should so like to give that room a good dusting, if it wouldn't vex them."

"My dear, they will probably never know the difference except by a vague sense of improved comfort. Men are dreadfully untidy, as a general thing, when left to themselves; but they like very well to have other people make things neat."

"Mr. Templestowe told Phil that they go off early in the morning and don't come back till breakfast at half-past seven; so if I wake early enough I shall try to do a little setting to rights before they come in."

"And I'll come and help if I don't over-sleep," declared Mrs. Hope; "but this air makes me feel dreadfully as if I should."

"I sha'n't call you," said Clover; "but it will be nice to have you, if you come."

She stood at her window after Mrs. Hope had gone, for a last look at the peak which glittered sharply in the light of the moon. The air was like scented wine. She drew a long breath.

"How lovely it is!" she said to herself, and kissed her hand to the mountain. "Good-night, you beautiful thing."

She woke with the first beam of yellow sun, after eight hours of dreamless sleep, with a keen sense of renovation and refreshment. A great splashing was going on in the opposite wing, and manly voices hushed to suppressed tones were audible. Then came a sound of boots on the porch; and peeping from behind her curtain, she saw Clarence and his friend striding across the grass in the direction of the stock-huts. She glanced at her watch. It was a quarter past five.

"Now is my chance," she thought; and dressing rapidly, she put on a little cambric jacket, knotted her hair up, tied a handkerchief over it, and hurried into the sitting-room. Her first act was to throw open all the windows to let out the smell of stale tobacco, her next to hunt for a broom. She found one at last, hanging on the door of a sort of store-closet, and moving the furniture as noiselessly as she could, she gave the room a rapid but effectual sweeping.

While the dust settled, she stole out to a place on the hillside where the night before she had noticed some mariposa lilies growing, and gathered a large bunch. Then she proceeded to dust and straighten, sorted out the newspapers, wiped the woodwork with a damp cloth, arranged the disorderly books, and set the breakfast-table. When all this was done, there was still time to finish her toilet and put her pretty hair in its accustomed coils and waves; so that Clarence and Mr. Templestowe came in to find the fire blazing, the room bright and neat, Mrs. Hope sitting at the table in a pretty violet gingham ready to pour the coffee which Choo Loo had brought in, and Clover, the good fairy of this transformation scene, in a fresh blue muslin, with a ribbon to match in her hair, just setting the mariposas in the middle of the table. Their lilac-streaked bells nodded from a tall vase of ground glass.

"Oh, I say," cried Clarence, "this *is* something like! Isn't it scrumptious, Geoff? The hut never looked like this before. It's wonderful what a woman— no, two women," with a bow to Mrs. Hope—"can do toward making things pleasant. Where did that vase come from, Clover? We never owned anything so fine as that, I'm sure."

"It came from my bag; and it's a present for you and Mr. Templestowe. I saw it in a shop-window yesterday; and it occurred to me that it might be just the thing for High Valley, and fill a gap. And Mrs. Hope has brought you each a pretty coffee-cup."

It was a merry meal. The pleasant look of the room, the little surprises, and the refreshment of seeing new and kindly faces, raised Mr. Templestowe's spirits, and warmed him out of his reserve. He grew cheerful and friendly. Clarence was in uproarious spirits, and Phil even worse. It seemed as if the air of the High Valley had got into his head.

Dr. Hope left at noon, after making a second visit to the lame herder, and Mrs. Hope and Clover settled themselves for a week of enjoyment. They were alone for hours every day, while their young hosts were off on the ranch, and they devoted part of this time to various useful and decorative arts. They took all manner of liberties, poked about and rummaged, mended, sponged, assorted, and felt themselves completely mistresses of the situation. A note to Marian Chase brought up a big parcel by stage to the Ute Valley, four miles away, from which it was fetched over by a cow-boy on horseback; and Clover worked away busily at scrim curtains for the windows, while Mrs. Hope shaped a slip cover of gay chintz for the shabbiest of the armchairs, hemmed a great square of gold-colored canton flannel for the bare, unsightly table, and made a bright red pincushion apiece for the bachelor quarters. The sitting-room took on quite a new aspect, and every added touch gave immense satisfaction to "the boys," as Mrs. Hope called them, who thoroughly enjoyed the effect of these ministrations, though they had not the least idea how to produce it themselves.

Creature comforts were not forgotten. The two ladies amused themselves with experiments in cookery. The herders brought a basket of wild raspberries, and Clover turned them into jam for winter use. Clarence gloated over the little white pots, and was never tired of counting them. They looked so like New England, he declared, that he felt as if he must get a girl at once, and go and walk in the graveyard,—a pastime which he remembered as universal in his native town. Various cakes and puddings appeared to attest the industry of the housekeepers; and on the only wet evening, when a wild thunder-gust was sweeping down the valley, they had a wonderful candy-pull, and made enough to give all the cow-boys a treat.

It must not be supposed that all their time went in these domestic pursuits. No, indeed. Mrs. Hope had brought her own side-saddle, and had borrowed one for Clover; the place was full of horses, and not a day passed without a long ride up or down the valley, and into the charming little side canyons which opened from it. A spirited broncho, named Sorrel, had been made over to Phil's use for the time of his stay, and he was never out of the saddle when he could help it, except to eat and sleep. He shared in the herders' wild gallops after stock, and though Clover felt nervous about the risks he ran, whenever she took time to think them over, he was so very happy that she had not the heart to interfere or check his pleasure.

She and Mrs. Hope rode out with the gentlemen on the great day of the round-up, and, stationed at a safe point a little way up the hillside, watched the spectacle,—the plunging, excited herd, the cow-boys madly galloping, swinging their long whips and lassos, darting to and fro to head off refractory beasts or check the tendency to stampede. Both Clarence and Geoffrey Templestowe were bold and expert riders; but the Mexican and Texan herders in their employ far surpassed them. The ladies had never seen anything like it. Phil and his broncho were in the midst of things, of course, and had one or two tumbles, but nothing to hurt them; only Clover was very thankful when it was all safely over.

In their rides and scrambling walks it generally happened that Clarence took possession of Clover, and left Geoff in charge of Mrs. Hope. Cousinship and old friendship gave him a right, he considered, and he certainly took full advantage of it. Clover liked Clarence; but there were moments when she felt that she would rather enjoy the chance to talk more with Mr. Templestowe, and there was a look in his eyes now and then which seemed to say that he might enjoy it too. But Clarence did not observe this look, and he had no idea of sharing his favorite cousin with any one, if he could help it.

Sunday brought the explanation of the shelf full of prayer-books which had puzzled them on their first arrival. There was no church within reach; and it was Geoff's regular custom, it seemed, to hold a little service for the men in the valley. Almost all of them came, except the few Mexicans, who were Roman Catholics, and the room was quite full. Geoff read the service well and reverently, gave out the hymns, and played the accompaniments for them, closing with a brief bit of a sermon by the elder Arnold. It was all done simply and as a matter of course, and Clarence seemed to join in it with much good-will; but Clover privately wondered whether the idea of doing such a thing would have entered into his head had he been left alone, or, if so, whether he would have cared enough about it to carry it out regularly. She doubted. Whatever the shortcomings of the Church of England may be, she certainly trains her children into a devout observance of Sunday.

The next day, Monday, was to be their last,—a fact lamented by every one, particularly Phil, who regarded the High Valley as a paradise, and would gladly have remained there for the rest of his natural life. Clover hated to take him away; but Dr. Hope had warned her privately that a week would be enough of it, and that with Phil's tendency to overdo, too long a stay would be undesirable. So she stood firm, though Clarence urged a delay, and Phil seconded the proposal with all his might.

The very pleasantest moment of the visit perhaps came on that last afternoon, when Geoff got her to himself for once, and took her up a trail where she had not yet been, in search of scarlet pentstemons to carry back to St. Helen's. They found great sheaves of the slender stems threaded, as it were, with jewel-like blossoms; but what was better still, they had a talk, and Clover felt that she had now a new friend. Geoff told her of his people at home, and a little about the sister who had lately died; only a little,—he could not yet trust himself to talk long about her. Clover listened with frank and gentle interest. She liked to hear about the old grange at the head of a chine above Clovelley, where Geoff was born, and which had once been full of boys and girls, now scattered in the English fashion to all parts of the world. There was Ralph with his regiment in India,—he was the heir, it seemed,—and Jim and Jack in Australia, and Oliver with his wife and children in New Zealand, and Allen at Harrow, and another boy fitting for the civil service. There was a married sister in Scotland, and another in London; and Isabel, the youngest of all, still at home,—the light of the house, and the special pet of the old squire and of Geoff's mother, who, he told Clover, had been a great beauty in her youth, and though nearly seventy, was in his eyes beautiful still.

"It's pretty quiet there for Isabel," he said; "but she has my sister Helen's two children to care for, and that will keep her busy. I used to think she'd come out to me one of these years for a twelvemonth; but there's little chance of her being spared now."

Clover's sympathy did not take the form of words. It looked out of her eyes, and spoke in the hushed tones of her soft voice. Geoff felt that it was there, and it comforted him. The poor fellow was very lonely in those days, and inclined to be homesick, as even a manly man sometimes is.

"What an awful time Adam must have had of it before Eve came!" growled Clarence, that evening, as they sat around the fire.

"He had a pretty bad time after she came, if I remember," said Clover, laughing.

"Ah, but he had *her*!"

"Stuff and nonsense! He was a long shot happier without her and her old apple, I think," put in Phil. "You fellows don't know when you're well off."

Everybody laughed.

"Phil's notion of Paradise is the High Valley and Sorrel, and no girls about to bother and tell him not to get too tired," remarked Clover. "It's a fair vision; but like all fair visions it must end."

And end it did next day, when Dr. Hope appeared with the carriage, and the bags and saddles were put in, and the great bundle of wild-flowers, with their stems tied in wet moss; and Phil, torn from his beloved broncho, on whose back he had passed so many happy hours, was forced to accompany the others back to civilization.

"I shall see you very soon," said Clarence, tucking the lap-robe round Clover. "There's the mail to fetch, and other things. I shall be riding in every day or two."

"I shall see you very soon," said Geoff, on the other side. "Clarence is not coming without me, I can assure you."

Then the carriage drove away; and the two partners went back into the house, which looked suddenly empty and deserted.

"I'll tell you what!" began Clarence.

"And I'll tell *you* what!" rejoined Geoff.

"A house isn't worth a red cent which hasn't a woman in it."

"You might ride down and ask Miss Perkins to step up and adorn our lives," said his friend, grimly. Miss Perkins was a particularly rigid spinster who taught a school six miles distant, and for whom Clarence entertained a particular distaste.

"You be hanged! I don't mean that kind. I mean—"

"The nice kind, like Mrs. Hope and your cousin. Well, I'm agreed."

"I shall go down after the mail to-morrow," remarked Clarence, between the puffs of his pipe.

"So shall I."

"All right; come along!" But though the words sounded hearty, the tone rather belied them. Clarence was a little puzzled by and did not quite like this newborn enthusiasm on the part of his comrade.

CHAPTER IX.

OVER A PASS.

True to their resolve, the young heads of the High Valley Ranch rode together to St. Helen's next day,—ostensibly to get their letters; in reality to call on their late departed guests. They talked amicably as they went; but unconsciously each was watching the other's mood and speech. To like the same girl makes young men curiously observant of each other.

A disappointment was in store for them. They had taken it for granted that Clover would be as disengaged and as much at their service as she had been in the valley; and lo! she sat on the piazza with a knot of girls about her, and a young man in an extremely "fetching" costume of snow-white duck, with a flower in his button-hole, was bending over her chair, and talking in a low voice of something which seemed of interest. He looked provokingly cool and comfortable to the dusty horsemen, and very much at home. Phil, who lounged against the piazza-rail opposite, dispensed an enormous and meaning wink at his two friends as they came up the steps.

Clover jumped up from her chair, and gave them a most cordial reception.

"How delightful to see you again so soon!" she said. Then she introduced them to a girl in pink and a girl in blue as Miss Perham and Miss Blanchard, and they shook hands with Marian Chase, whom they already knew, and lastly were presented to Mr. Wade, the youth in white. The three young men eyed one another with a not very friendly scrutiny, just veiled by the necessary outward politeness.

"Then you will be all ready for Thursday,—and your brother too, of course,—and my mother will stop for you at half-past ten on her way down," they heard him say. "Miss Chase will go with the Hopes. Oh, yes; there will be plenty of room. No danger about that. We're almost sure to have good weather too. Good-morning. I'm so glad you enjoyed the roses."

There was a splendid cluster of Jacqueminot buds in Clover's dress, at which Clarence glared wrathfully as he caught these words. The only consolation was that the creature in duck was going. He was making his last bows; and one of the girls went with him, which still farther reduced the number of what in his heart Clarence stigmatized as "a crowd."

"I must go too," said the girl in blue. "Good-by, Clover. I shall run in a minute to-morrow to talk over the last arrangements for Thursday."

"What's going to happen on Thursday?" growled Clarence as soon as she had departed.

"Oh, such a delightful thing," cried Clover, sparkling and dimpling. "Old Mr. Wade, the father of young Mr. Wade, whom you saw just now, is a director on the railroad, you know; and they have given him the director's car to take a party over the Marshall Pass, and he has asked Phil and me to go. It is *such* a surprise. Ever since we came to St. Helen's, people have been telling us what a beautiful journey it is; but I never supposed we should have the chance to take it. Mrs.

Hope is going too, and the doctor, and Miss Chase and Miss Perham,—all the people we know best, in fact. Isn't it nice?"

"Oh, certainly; very nice," replied Clarence, in a tone of deep offence. He was most unreasonably in the sulks. Clover glanced at him with surprise, and then at Geoff, who was talking to Marian. He looked a little serious, and not so bright as in the valley; but he was making himself very pleasant, notwithstanding. Surely he had the same causes for annoyance as Clarence; but his breeding forbade him to show whatever inward vexation he may have felt,—certainly not to allow it to influence his manners. Clover drew a mental contrast between the two which was not to Clarence's advantage.

"Who's that fellow anyway?" demanded Clarence. "How long have you known him? What business has he to be bringing you roses, and making up parties to take you off on private cars?"

Something in Clover's usually soft eyes made him stop suddenly.

"I beg your pardon," he said in an altered tone.

"I really think you should," replied Clover, with pretty dignity.

Then she moved away, and began to talk to Geoff, whose grave courtesy at once warmed into cheer and sun.

Clarence, thus left a prey to remorse, was wretched. He tried to catch Clover's eye, but she wouldn't look at him. He leaned against the balustrade moody and miserable. Phil, who had watched these various interludes with interest, indicated his condition to Clover with another telegraphic wink. She glanced across, relented, and made Clarence a little signal to come and sit by her.

After that all went happily. Clover was honestly delighted to see her two friends again. And now that Clarence had recovered from his ill-temper, there was nothing to mar their enjoyment. Geoff's horse had cast a shoe on the way down, it seemed, and must be taken to the blacksmith's, so they did not stay very long; but it was arranged that they should come back to dinner at Mrs. Marsh's.

"What a raving belle you are!" remarked Marian Chase, as the young men rode away. "Three is a good many at a time, though, isn't it?"

"Three what?"

"Three—hem! leaves—to one Clover!"

"It's the usual allowance, I believe. If there were four, now—"

"Oh, I dare say there will be. They seem to collect round you like wasps round honey. It's some natural law, I presume,—gravitation or levitation, which is it?"

"I'm sure I don't know, and don't try to tease me, Poppy. People out here are so kind that it's enough to spoil anybody."

"Kind, forsooth! Do you consider it all pure kindness? Really, for such a belle, you're very innocent."

"I wish you wouldn't," protested Clover, laughing and coloring. "I never was a belle in my life, and that's the second time you've called me that. Nobody ever said such things to me in Burnet."

"Ah, you had to come to Colorado to find out how attractive you could be. Burnet must be a very quiet place. Never mind; you sha'n't be teased, Clover dear. Only don't let this trefoil of yours get to fighting with one another. That good-looking cousin of yours was casting quite murderous glances at poor Thurber Wade just now."

"Clarence is a dear boy; but he's rather spoiled and not quite grown up yet, I think."

"When are you coming back from the Marshall Pass?" inquired Geoff, after dinner, when Clarence had gone for the horses.

"On Saturday. We shall only be gone two days."

"Then I will ride in on Thursday morning, if you will permit, with my field-glass. It is a particularly good one, and you may find it useful for the distant views."

"When are you coming back?" demanded Clarence, a little later. "Saturday? Then I sha'n't be in again before Monday."

"Won't you want your letters?"

"Oh, I guess there won't be any worth coming for till then."

"Not a letter from your mother?"

"She only writes once in a while. Most of what I get comes from pa."

"Cousin Olivia never did seem to care much for Clarence," remarked Clover, after they were gone. "He would have been a great deal nicer if he had had a pleasanter time at home. It makes such a difference with boys. Now Mr. Templestowe has a lovely mother, I'm sure."

"Oh!" was all the reply that Phil would vouchsafe.

"How queer people are!" thought little Clover to herself afterward. "Neither of those boys quite liked our going on this expedition, I think,—though I'm sure I can't imagine why; but they behaved so differently. Mr. Templestowe thought of us and something which might give us pleasure; and Clarence only thought about himself. Poor Clarence! he never had half a chance till he came here. It isn't all his fault."

The party in the director's car proved a merry one. Mrs. Wade, a jolly, motherly woman, fond of the good things of life, and delighting in making people comfortable, had spared no pains of preparation. There were quantities of easy-chairs and fans and eau-de-cologne; the larder was stocked with all imaginable dainties,—iced tea, lemonade, and champagne cup flowed on the least provocation for all the hot moments, and each table was a bank of flowers. Each lady had a superb bouquet; and on the second day a great tin box of freshly-cut roses met them at Pueblo, so that they came back as gayly furnished forth as they went. Having the privilege of the road, the car was attached or detached to suit their convenience, and this enabled them to command daylight for all the finest points of the excursion.

First of these was the Royal Gorge, where the Arkansas River pours through a magnificent canyon, between precipices so steep and with curves so sharp that only engineering genius of the most daring order could, it would seem, have devised a way through. Then, after a pause at the pretty town of Salida, with the magnificent range of the Sangre de Cristo Mountains in full sight, they began to mount the pass over long loops of rail, which doubled and re-doubled on themselves again and again on their way to the summit. The train had been divided; and the first half with its two engines was seen at times puffing and snorting directly overhead of the second half on the lower curve.

With each hundred feet of elevation, the view changed and widened. Now it was of over-lapping hills set with little mésas, like folds of green velvet flung over the rocks; now of dim-seen valley depths with winding links of silver rivers; and again of countless mountain peaks sharp-cut against the sunset sky,—some rosy pink, some shining with snow.

The flowers were a continual marvel. At the top of the pass, eleven thousand feet and more above the sea, their colors and their abundance were more profuse and splendid than on the lower levels. There were whole fields of pentstemons, pink, blue, royal purple, or the rare scarlet variety, like stems of asparagus strung with rubies. There were masses of gillias, and of wonderful coreopsis, enormous cream-colored stars with deep-orange centres, and deep yellow ones with scarlet centres; thickets of snowy-cupped mentzelia and of wild rose; while here and there a tall red lily burned like a little lonely flame in the green, or regiments of convolvuli waved their stately heads.

From below came now and again the tinkle of distant cow-bells. These, and the plaintive coo of mourning-doves in the branches, and the rush of the wind, which was like cool flower-scented wine, was all that broke the stillness of the high places.
"To think I'm so much nearer heaven
Than when I was a boy,"
misquoted Clover, as she sat on the rear platform of the car, with Poppy, and Thurber Wade.

"Are you sure your head doesn't ache? This elevation plays the mischief with some people. My mother has taken to her berth with ice on her temples."

"Headache! No, indeed. This air is too delicious. I feel as though I could dance all the way from here to the Black Canyon."

"You don't look as if your head ached, or anything," said Mr. Wade, staring at Clover admiringly. Her cheeks were pink with excitement, her eyes full of light and exhilaration.

"Oh dear! we are beginning to go down," she cried, watching one of the beautiful peaks of the Sangre de Cristos as it dipped out of sight. "I think I could find it in my heart to cry, if it were not that to-morrow we are coming up again."

So down, down, down they went. Dusk slowly gathered about them; and the white-gloved butler set the little tables, and brought in broiled chicken and grilled salmon and salad and hot rolls and peaches, and they were all very hungry. And Clover did not cry, but fell to work on her supper with an excellent appetite, quite unconscious that they were speeding through another wonderful gorge without seeing one of its beauties. Then the car was detached from the train; and when she awoke next morning they were at the little station called Cimmaro, at the head of the famous Black Canyon, with three hours to spare before the train from Utah should arrive to take them back to St. Helen's.

Early as it was, the small settlement was awake. Lights glanced from the eating-house, where cooks were preparing breakfast for the "through" passengers, and smokes curled from the chimneys. Close to the car was a large brick structure which seemed to be a sort of hotel for locomotives. A number of the enormous creatures had evidently passed the night there, and just waked up. Clover now watched their antics with great amusement from her window as their engineers ran them in and out, rubbed them down like horses, and fed them with oil and coal, while they snorted and backed and sidled a good deal as real horses do. Clover could not at all understand what all these manoeuvres were for,—they seemed only designed to show the paces of the iron steeds, and what they were good for.

"Miss Clover," whispered a voice outside her curtains, "I've got hold of a hand-car and a couple of men; and don't you want to take a spin down the canyon and see the view with no smoke to spoil it? Just you and me and Miss Chase. She says she'll go if you will. Hurry, and don't make a noise. We won't wake the others."

Of course Clover wanted to. She finished her dressing at top-speed, hurried on her hat and jacket, stole softly out to where the others awaited her, and in five minutes they were smoothly running down the gorge, over high trestle-work bridges and round sharp curves which made her draw her breath a little faster. There was no danger, the men who managed the hand-car assured them; it was a couple of hours yet before the next train came in; there was plenty of time to go three or four miles down and return.

Anything more delicious than the early morning air in the Black Canyon it would be difficult to imagine. Cool, odorous with pines and with the breath of the mountains, it was like a zestful draught of iced summer. Close beside the track ran a wondrous river which seemed made of melted jewels, so curiously brilliant were its waters and mixed of so many hues. Its course among the rocks was a flash of foaming rapids, broken here and there by pools of exquisite blue-green, deepening into inky-violet under the shadow of the cliffs. And such cliffs!—one, two, three thousand feet high; not deep-colored like those about St. Helen's, but of steadfast mountain hues and of magnificent forms,—buttresses and spires; crags whose bases were lost in untrodden forests; needle-sharp pinnacles like the Swiss Aiguilles. The morning was just making its way into the canyon; and the loftier tops flashed with yellow sun, while the rest were still in cold shadow.

Breakfast was just ready when the hand-car arrived again at the upper end of the gorge, and loud were the reproaches which met the happy three as they alighted from it. Phil was particularly afflicted.

"I call it mean not to wake a fellow," he said.

"But a fellow was *so* sound asleep," said Clover, "I really hadn't the heart. I did peep in at your curtain, and if you had moved so much as a finger, *perhaps* I should have called you; but you didn't."

The return journey was equally fortunate, and the party reached St. Helen's late in the evening of the second day, in what Mr. Wade called "excellent form."

Monday brought the young men from the ranch in again; and another fortnight passed happily, Clover's three "leaves" being most faithfully attentive to their central point of attraction. "Three is a good many," as Marian Chase had said, but all girls like to be liked, and Clover did not find this, her first little experience of the kind, at all disagreeable.

The excursion to the Marshall Pass, however, had an after effect which was not so pleasant. Either the high elevation had disagreed with Phil, or he had taken a little cold; at all events, he was distinctly less well. With the lowering of his physical forces came a corresponding depression of spirits. Mrs. Watson worried him, the sick people troubled him, the sound of coughing depressed him, his appetite nagged, and his sleep was broken. Clover felt that he must have a change, and consulted Dr. Hope, who advised their going to the Ute Valley for a month.

This involved giving up their rooms at Mrs. Marsh's, which was a pity, as it was by no means certain that they would be able to get them again later. Clover regretted this; but Fate, as Fate often does, brought a compensation. Mrs. Watson had no mind whatever for the Ute Valley.

"It's a dull place, they tell me, and there's nothing to do there but ride on horseback, and as I don't ride on horseback, I really don't see what use there would be in my going," she said to Clover. "If I were young, and there were young men ready to ride with me all the time, it would be different; though Ellen never did care to, except with Henry of course, after they—And I really can't see that your brother's much different from what he was, though if Dr. Hope says so, naturally you—He's a queer kind of doctor, it seems to me, to send lung patients up higher than this,—which is high already, gracious knows. No; if you decide to go, I shall just move over to the Shoshone for the rest of the time that I'm here. I'm sure that Dr. Carr couldn't expect me to stay on here alone, just for the chance that you may want to come back, when as like as not, Mrs. Marsh won't be able to take you again."

"Oh, no; I'm quite sure he wouldn't. Only I thought," doubtfully, "that as you've always admired Phil's room so much, you might like to secure it now that we have to go."

"Well, yes. If you were to be here, I might. If that man who's so sick had got better, or gone away, or something, I dare say I should have settled down in his room and been comfortable enough. But he seems just about as he was when we came, so there's no use waiting; and I'd rather go to the Shoshone anyway. I always said it was a mistake that we didn't go there in the first place. It was Dr. Hope's doing, and I have not the least confidence in him. He hasn't osculated me once since I came."

"Hasn't he?" said Clover, feeling her voice tremble, and perfectly aware of the shaking of Phil's shoulders behind her.

"No; and I don't call just putting his ear to my chest, listening. Dr. Bangs, at home, would be ashamed to come to the house without his stethoscope. I mean to move this afternoon. I've given Mrs. Marsh notice."

So Mrs. Watson and her belongings went to the Shoshone, and Clover packed the trunks with a lighter heart for her departure.

The last day of July found Clover and Phil settled in the Ute Park. It was a wild and beautiful valley, some hundreds of feet higher than St. Helen's, and seemed the very home of peace. A Sunday-like quiet pervaded the place, whose stillness was never broken except by bird-songs and the rustle of the pine branches.

The sides of the valley near its opening were dotted here and there with huts and cabins belonging to parties who had fled from the heat of the plains for the summer. At the upper end stood the ranch house,—a large, rather rudely built structure,—and about it were a number of cabins and cottages, in which two, four, or six people could be accommodated. Clover and Phil were lodged in one of these. The tiny structure contained only a sitting and two sleeping rooms, and was very plain and bare. But there was a fireplace; wood was abundant, so that a cheerful blaze could be had for cool evenings; and the little piazza faced the south, and made a sheltered sitting place on windy days.

One pleasant feature of the spot was its nearness to the High Valley. Clarence and Geoff Templestowe thought nothing of riding four miles; and scarcely a day passed when one or both did not come over. They brought wild-flowers, or cream, or freshly-churned butter, as offerings from the ranch; and, what Clover valued as a greater kindness yet, they brought Phil's beloved broncho, Sorrel, and arranged with the owner of the Ute ranch that it should remain as long as Phil was there. This gave Phil hours of delightful exercise every day; and though sometimes he set out early in the morning for the High Valley, and stayed later in the afternoon than his sister thought prudent, she had not the heart to chide, so long as he was visibly getting better hour by hour.

Sundays the friends spent together, as a matter of course. Geoff waited till his little home service for the ranchmen was over, and then would gallop across with Clarence to pass the rest of the day. There was no lack of kind people at the main house and in the cottages to take an interest in the delicate boy and his sweet, motherly sister; so Clover had an abundance of volunteer matrons, and plenty of pleasant ways in which to spend those occasional days on which the High Valley attaches failed to appear.

It was a simple, healthful life, the happiest on the whole which they had led since leaving home. Once or twice Mr. Thurber Wade made his appearance, gallantly mounted, and freighted with flowers and kind messages from his mother to Miss Carr; but Clover was never sorry when he rode away again. Somehow he did not seem to belong to the Happy Valley, as in her heart she denominated the place.

There was a remarkable deal of full moon that month, as it seemed; at least, the fact served as an excuse for a good many late transits between the valley and the park. Now and then either Clarence or Geoff would lead over a saddle-horse and give Clover a good gallop up or down the valley, which she always enjoyed. The habit which she had extemporized for her visit to the High Valley answered very well, and Mrs. Hope had lent her a hat.

On one of these occasions she and Clarence had ridden farther than usual, quite down to the end of the pass, where the road dipped, and descended to the little watering-place of Canyon Creek,—a Swiss-like village of hotels and lodging-houses and shops for the sale of minerals and mineral waters, set along the steep sides of a narrow green valley. They were chatting gayly, and had just agreed that it was time to turn their horses' heads homeward, when a sudden darkening made them aware that one of the unexpected thunder-gusts peculiar to the region was upon them.

They were still a mile above the village; but as no nearer place of shelter presented itself, they decided to proceed. But the storm moved more rapidly than they; and long before the first houses came in sight the heavy drops began to pelt down. A brown young fellow, lying flat on his back under a thick bush, with his horse standing over him, shouted to them to "try the cave," waving his hand in its direction; and hurrying on, they saw in another moment a shelving brow of rock in the cliff, under which was a deep recess.

To this Clarence directed the horses. He lifted Clover down. She half sat, half leaned on the slope of the rock, well under cover, while he stretched himself at full length on a higher ledge, and held the bridles fast. The horses' heads and the saddles were fairly well protected, but the hindquarters of the animals were presently streaming with water.

"This isn't half-bad, is it?" Clarence said. His mouth was so close to Clover's ear that she could catch his words in spite of the noisy thunder and the roar of the descending rain.

"No; I call it fun."

"You look awfully pretty, do you know?" was the next and very unexpected remark.

"Nonsense."

"Not nonsense at all."

At that moment a carriage dashed rapidly by, the driver guiding the horses as well as he could between the points of an umbrella, which constantly menaced his eyes. Other travellers in the pass had evidently been surprised by the storm besides themselves. The lady who held the umbrella looked out, and caught the picture of the group under the cliff. It was a suggestive one. Clover's hat was a little pushed forward by the rock against which she leaned, which in its turn pushed forward the waving rings of hair which shaded her forehead, but did not hide her laughing eyes, or the dimples in her pink cheeks. The fair, slender girl, the dark, stalwart young fellow so close to her, the rain, the half-sheltered horses,—it was easy enough to construct a little romance.

The lady evidently did so. It was what photographers call an "instantaneous effect," caught in three seconds, as the carriage whirled past; but in that fraction of a minute the lady had nodded and flashed a brilliant, sympathetic smile in their direction, and Clover had nodded in return, and laughed back.

"A good many people seem to have been caught as we have," she said, as another streaming vehicle dashed by.

"I wish it would rain for a week," observed Clarence.

"My gracious, what a wish! What would become of us if it did?"

"We should stay here just where we are, and I should have you all to myself for once, and nobody could come in to interfere with me."

"Thank you extremely! How hungry we should be! How can you be so absurd, Clarence?"

"I'm not absurd at all. I'm perfectly in earnest."

"Do you mean that you really want to stay a week under this rock with nothing to eat?"

"Well, no; not exactly that perhaps,—though if you could, I would. But I mean that I would like to get you for a whole solid week to myself. There is such a gang of people about always, and they all want you. Clover," he went on, for, puzzled at his tone, she made no answer, "couldn't you like me a little?"

"I like you a great deal. You come next to Phil and Dorry with me."

"Hang Phil and Dorry! Who wants to come next to them? I want you to like me a great deal more than that. I want you to love me. Couldn't you, Clover?"

"How strangely you talk! I do love you, of course. You're my cousin."

"I don't care to be loved 'of course.' I want to be loved for myself. Clover, you know what I mean; you must know. I can afford to marry now; won't you stay in Colorado and be my wife?"

"I don't think you know what you are saying, Clarence. I'm older than you are. I thought you looked upon me as a sort of mother or older sister."

"Only fifteen months older," retorted Clarence. "I never heard of any one's being a mother at that age. I'm a man now, I would have you remember, though I am a little younger than you, and know my own mind as well as if I were fifty. Dear Clovy," coaxingly, "couldn't you? You liked the High Valley, didn't you? I'd do anything possible to make it nice and pleasant for you."

"I do like the High Valley very much," said Clover, still with the feeling that Clarence must be half in joke, or she half in dream. "But, my dear boy, it isn't my home. I couldn't leave papa and the children, and stay out here, even with you. It would seem so strange and far away."

"You could if you cared for me," replied Clarence, dejectedly; Clover's kind, argumentative, elder-sisterly tone was precisely that which is most discouraging to a lover.

"Oh, dear," cried poor Clover, not far from tears herself; "this is dreadful!"

"What?" moodily. "Having an offer? You must have had lots of them before now."

"Indeed I never did. People don't do such things in Burnet. Please don't say any more, Clarence. I'm very fond of you, just as I am of the boys; but—"

"But what? Go on."

"How can I?" Clover was fairly crying.

"You mean that you can't love me in the other way."

"Yes." The word came out half as a sob, but the sincerity of the accent was unmistakable.

"Well," said poor Clarence, after a long bitter pause; "it isn't your fault, I suppose. I'm not good enough for you. Still, I'd have done my best, if you would have taken me, Clover."

"I am sure you would," eagerly. "You've always been my favorite cousin, you know. People can't *make* themselves care for each other; it has to come in spite of them or not at all,—at least, that is what the novels say. But you're not angry with me, are you, dear? We will be good friends always, sha'n't we?" persuasively.

"I wonder if we can," said Clarence, in a hopeless tone. "It doesn't seem likely; but I don't know any more about it than you do. It's my first offer as well as yours." Then, after a silence and a struggle, he added in a more manful tone, "We'll try for it, at least. I can't afford to give you up. You're the sweetest girl in the world. I always said so, and I say so still. It will be hard at first, but perhaps it may grow easier with time."

"Oh, it will," cried Clover, hopefully. "It's only because you're so lonely out here, and see so few people, that makes you suppose I am better than the rest. One of these days you'll find a girl who is a great deal nicer than I am, and then you'll be glad that I didn't say yes. There! the rain is just stopping."

"It's easy enough to talk," remarked Clarence, gloomily, as he gathered up the bridles of the horses; "but I shall do nothing of the kind. I declare I won't!"

CHAPTER X.

NO. 13 PIUTE STREET.

Clover did not see Clarence again for several days after this conversation, the remembrance of which was uncomfortable to her. She feared he was feeling hurt or "huffy," and would show it in his manner; and she disliked very much the idea that Phil might suspect the reason, or, worse still, Mr. Templestowe.

But when he finally appeared he seemed much the same as usual. After all, she reflected, it has only been a boyish impulse; he has already got over it, or not meant all he said.

In this she did Clarence an injustice. He had been very much in earnest when he spoke; and it showed the good stuff which was in him and his real regard for Clover that he should be making so manly a struggle with his disappointment and pain. His life had been a lonely one in Colorado; he could not afford to quarrel with his favorite cousin, and with him, as with other lovers, there may have been, besides, some lurking hope that she might yet change her mind. But perhaps Clover in a measure was right in her conviction that Clarence was still too young and undeveloped to have things go very deep with him. He seemed to her in many ways as boyish and as undisciplined as Phil.

With early September the summering of the Ute Park came to a close. The cold begins early at that elevation, and light frosts and red leaves warned the dwellers in tents and cabins to flee.

Clover made her preparations for departure with real reluctance. She had grown very fond of the place; but Phil was perfectly himself again, and there seemed no reason for their staying longer.

So back to St. Helen's they went and to Mrs. Marsh, who, in reply to Clover's letter, had written that she must make room for them somehow, though for the life of her she couldn't say how. It proved to be in two small back rooms. An irruption of Eastern invalids had filled the house to overflowing, and new faces met them at every turn. Two or three of the last summer's inmates had died during their stay,—one of them the very sick man whose room Mrs. Watson had coveted. His death took place "as if on purpose," she told Clover, the very week after her removal to the Shoshone.

Mrs. Watson herself was preparing for return to the East. "I've seen the West now," she said,—"all I want to see; and I'm quite ready to go back to my own part of the country. Ellen writes that she thinks I'd better start for home so as to get settled before the cold—And it's so cold here that I can't realize that they're still in the middle of peaches at home. Ellen always spices a great— They're better than preserves; and as for the canned ones, why, peaches and water is what I call them. Well—my dear—" (Distance lends enchantment, and Clover had become "My dear" again.) "I'm glad I could come out and help you along; and now that you know so many people here, you won't need me so much as you did at first. I shall tell Mrs. Perkins to write to Mrs. Hall to tell your father how well your brother is looking, and I know he'll be—And here's a little handkerchief for a keepsake."

It was a pretty handkerchief, of pale yellow silk with embroidered corners, and Clover kissed the old lady as she thanked her, and they parted good friends. But their intercourse had led her to make certain firm resolutions.

"I will try to keep my mind clear and my talk clear; to learn what I want and what I have a right to want and what I mean to say, so as not to puzzle and worry people when I grow old, by being vague and helpless and fussy," she reflected. "I suppose if I don't form the habit now, I sha'n't be able to then, and it would be dreadful to end by being like poor Mrs. Watson."

Altogether, Mrs. Marsh's house had lost its homelike character; and it was not strange that under the circumstances Phil should flag a little. He was not ill, but he was out of sorts and dismal, and disposed to consider the presence of so many strangers as a personal wrong. Clover felt that it was not a good atmosphere for him, and anxiously revolved in her mind what was best to do. The Shoshone was much too expensive; good boarding-houses in St. Helen's were few and far between, and all of them shared in a still greater degree the disadvantages which had made themselves felt at Mrs. Marsh's.

The solution to her puzzle came—as solutions often do—unexpectedly. She was walking down Piute Street on her way to call on Alice Blanchard, when her attention was attracted to a small, shut-up house, on which was a sign: "No. 13. To Let, Furnished." The sign was not printed, but written on a half-sheet of foolscap, which was what led Clover to notice it.

She studied the house a while, then opened the gate, and went in. Two or three steps led to a little piazza. She seated herself on the top step, and tried to peep in at the closed blinds of the nearest window.

While she was doing so, a woman with a shawl over her head came hastily down a narrow side street or alley, and approached her.

"Oh, did you want the key?" she said.

"The key?" replied Clover, surprised; "of this house, do you mean?"

"Yes. Mis Starkey left it with me when she went away, because, she said, it was handy, and I could give it to anybody who wished to look at the place. You're the first that has come; so when I see you setting here, I just ran over. Did Mr. Beloit send you?"

"No; nobody sent me. Is it Mr. Beloit who has the letting of the house?"

"Yes; but I can let folks in. I told Mis Starkey I'd air and dust a little now and then, if it wasn't took. Poor soul! she was anxious enough about it; and it all had to be done on a sudden, and she in such a heap of trouble that she didn't know which way to turn. It was just lock-up and go!"

"Tell me about her," said Clover, making room on the step for the woman to sit down.

"Well, she come out last year with her man, who had lung trouble, and he wasn't no better at first, and then he seemed to pick up for a while; and they took this house and fixed themselves to stay for a year, at least. They made it real nice, too, and slicked up considerable. Mis Starkey said, said she, 'I don't want to spend no more money on it than I can help, but Mr. Starkey must be made comfortable,' says she, them was her very words. He used to set out on this stoop all day long in the summer, and she alongside him, except when she had to be indoors doing the work. She didn't keep no regular help. I did the washing for her, and come in now and then for a day to clean; so she managed very well.

"Then,—Wednesday before last, it was,—he had a bleeding, and sank away like all in a minute, and was gone before the doctor could be had. Mis Starkey was all stunned like with the shock of it; and before she had got her mind cleared up so's to order about anything, come a telegraph to say her son was down with diphtheria, and his wife with a young baby, and both was very low. And between one and the other she was pretty near out of her wits. We packed her up as quick as we could, and he was sent off by express; and she says to me, 'Mis Kenny, you see how 't is. I've got this house on my hands till May. There's no time to see to anything, and I've got no heart to care; but if any one'll take it for the winter, well and good; and I'll leave the sheets and table-cloths and everything in it, because it may make a difference, and I don't mind about them nohow. And if no one does take it, I'll just have to bear the loss,' says she. Poor soul! she was in a world of trouble, surely."

"Do you know what rent she asks for the house?" said Clover, in whose mind a vague plan was beginning to take shape.

"Twenty-five a month was what she paid; and she said she'd throw the furniture in for the rest of the time, just to get rid of the rent."

Clover reflected. Twenty-five dollars a week was what they were paying at Mrs. Marsh's. Could they take this house and live on the same sum, after deducting the rent, and perhaps get this good-natured-looking woman to come in for a certain number of hours and help do the work? She almost fancied that they could if they kept no regular servant.

"I think I *would* like to see the house," she said at last, after a silent calculation and a scrutinizing look at Mrs. Kenny, who was a faded, wiry, but withal kindly-looking person, shrewd and clean,—a North of Ireland Protestant, as she afterward told Clover. In fact, her accent was rather Scotch than Irish.

They went in. The front door opened into a minute hall, from which another door led into a back hall with a staircase. There was a tiny sitting-room, an equally tiny dining-room, a small kitchen, and above, two bedrooms and a sort of unplastered space, which would answer to put trunks in. That was all, save a little woodshed. Everything was bare and scanty and rather particularly ugly. The sitting-room had a frightful paper of mingled mustard and molasses tint, and a matted floor; but there was a good-sized open fireplace for the burning of wood, in which two bricks did duty for andirons, three or four splint and cane bottomed chairs, a lounge, and a table, while the pipe of the large "Morning-glory" stove in the dining-room expanded into a sort of drum in the chamber above. This secured a warm sleeping place for Phil. Clover began to think that they could make it do.

Mrs. Kenny, who evidently considered the house as a wonder of luxury and convenience, opened various cupboards, and pointed admiringly to the glass and china, the kitchen tins and utensils, and the cotton sheets and pillow-cases which they respectively held.

"There's water laid on," she said; "you don't have to pump any. Here's the washtubs in the shed. That's a real nice tin boiler for the clothes,—I never see a nicer. Mis Starkey had that heater in the dining-room set the very week before she went away. 'Winter's coming on,' she says, 'and I must see about keeping my husband warm;' never thinking, poor thing, how 't was to be."

"Does this chimney draw?" asked the practical Clover; "and does the kitchen stove bake well?"

"First-rate. I've seen Mis Starkey take her biscuits out many a time,—as nice a brown as ever you'd want; and the chimney don't smoke a mite. They kep' a wood fire here in May most all the time, so I know."

Clover thought the matter over for a day or two, consulted with Dr. Hope, and finally decided to try the experiment. No. 13 was taken, and Mrs. Kenny engaged for two days' work each week, with such other occasional assistance as Clover might require. She was a widow, it seemed, with one son, who, being employed on the railroad, only came home for the nights. She was glad of a regular engagement, and proved an excellent stand-by and a great help to Clover, to whom she had taken a fancy from the start; and many were the good turns which she did for love rather than hire for "my little Miss," as she called her.

To Phil the plan seemed altogether delightful. This was natural, as all the fun fell to his share and none of the trouble; a fact of which Mrs. Hope occasionally reminded him. Clover persisted, however, that it was all fair, and that she got lots of fun out of it too, and didn't mind the trouble. The house was so absurdly small that it seemed to strike every one as a good joke; and Clover's friends set themselves to help in the preparations, as if the establishment in Piute Street were a kind of baby-house about which they could amuse themselves at will.

It is a temptation always to make a house pretty, but Clover felt herself on honor to spend no more than was necessary. Papa had trusted her, and she was resolved to justify his trust. So she bravely withstood her desire for several things which would have been great improvements so far as looks went, and confined her purchases to articles of clear necessity,—extra blankets, a bedside carpet for Phil's room, and a chafing-dish over which she could prepare little impromptu dishes, and so save fuel and fatigue. She allowed herself some cheap Madras curtains for the parlor, and a few yards of deep-red flannel to cover sundry shelves and corner brackets which Geoffrey Templestowe, who had a turn for carpentry, put up for her. Various loans and gifts, too, appeared from friendly attics and store-rooms to help out. Mrs. Hope hunted up some old iron firedogs and a pair of bellows, Poppy contributed a pair of brass-knobbed tongs, and Mrs. Marsh lent her a lamp. No. 13 began to look attractive.

They were nearly ready, but not yet moved in, when one day as Clover stood in the queer little parlor, contemplating the effect of Geoff's last effort,—an extra pine shelf above the narrow mantel-shelf,—a pair of arms stole round her waist, and a cheek which had a sweet familiarity about it was pressed against hers. She turned, and gave a great shriek of amazement and joy, for it was her sister Katy's arms that held her. Beyond, in the doorway, were Mrs. Ashe and Amy, with Phil between them.

"Is it you; is it really you?" cried Clover, laughing and sobbing all at once in her happy excitement. "How did it happen? I never knew that you were coming."

"Neither did we; it all happened suddenly," explained Katy. "The ship was ordered to New York on three days' notice, and as soon as Ned sailed, Polly and I made haste to follow. There would have been just time to get a letter here if we had written at once, but I had the fancy to give you a surprise."

"Oh, it is *such* a nice surprise! But when did you come, and where are you?"

"At the Shoshone House,—at least our bags are there; but we only stayed a minute, we were in such a hurry to get to you. We went to Mrs. Marsh's and found Phil, who brought us here. Have you really taken this funny little house, as Phil tells us?"

"We really have. Oh, what a comfort it will be to tell you all about it, and have you say if I have done right! Dear, dear Katy, I feel as if home had just arrived by train. And Polly, too! You all look so well, and as if California had agreed with you. Amy has grown so that I should scarcely have known her."

Four delightful days followed. Katy flung herself into all Clover's plans with the full warmth of sisterly interest; and though the Hopes and other kind friends made many hospitable overtures, and would gladly have turned her short visit into a continuous *fête*, she persisted in keeping the main part of her time free. She must see a little of St. Helen's, she declared, so as to be able to tell her father about it, and she must help Clover to get to housekeeping,—these were the important things, and nothing else must interfere with them.

Most effectual assistance did she render in the way of unpacking and arranging. More than that, one day, when Clover, rather to her own disgust, had been made to go with Polly and Amy to Denver while Katy stayed behind, lo! on her return, a transformation had taken place, and the ugly paper in the parlor of No. 13 was found replaced with one of warm, sunny gold-brown.

"Oh, why did you?" cried Clover. "It's only for a few months, and the other would have answered perfectly well. Why did you, Katy?"

"I suppose it *was* foolish," Katy admitted; "but somehow I couldn't bear to have you sitting opposite that deplorable mustard-colored thing all winter long. And really and truly it hardly cost anything. It was a remnant reduced to ten cents a roll,—the whole thing was less than four dollars. You can call it your Christmas present from me, if you like, and I shall 'play' besides that the other paper had arsenic in it; I'm sure it looked as if it had, and corrosive sublimate, too."

Clover laughed outright. It was so funny to hear Katy's fertility of excuse.

"You dear, ridiculous darling!" she said, giving her sister a good hug; "it was just like you, and though I scold I am perfectly delighted. I did hate that paper with all my heart, and this is lovely. It makes the room look like a different thing."

Other benefactions followed. Polly, it appeared, had bought more Indian curiosities in Denver than she knew what to do with, and begged permission to leave a big bear-skin and two wolf-skins with Clover for the winter, and a splendid striped Navajo blanket as a portière to keep off draughts from the entry. Katy had set herself up in California blankets while they were in San Francisco, and she now insisted on leaving a pair behind, and loaning Clover besides one of two beautiful Japanese silk pictures which Ned had given her, and which made a fine spot of color on the pretty new wall. There were presents in her trunks for all at home, and Ned had sent Clover a beautiful lacquered box.

Somehow Clover seemed like a new and doubly-interesting Clover to Katy. She was struck by the self-reliance which had grown upon her, by her bright ways and the capacity and judgment which all her arrangements exhibited; and she listened with delight to Mrs. Hope's praises of her sister.

"She really is a wonderful little creature; so wise and judgmatical, and yet so pretty and full of fun. People are quite cracked about her out here. I don't think you'll ever get her back at the East again, Mrs. Worthington. There seems a strong determination on the part of several persons to keep her here."

"What do you mean?"

But Mrs. Hope, who believed in the old proverb about not addling eggs by meddling with them prematurely, refused to say another word. Clover, when questioned, "could not imagine what Mrs. Hope meant;" and Katy had to go away with her curiosity unsatisfied. Clarence came in once while she was there, but she did not see Mr. Templestowe.

Katy's last gift to Clover was a pretty tea-pot of Japanese ware. "I meant it for Cecy," she explained. "But as you have none I'll give it to you instead, and take her the fan I meant for you. It seems more appropriate."

Phil and Clover moved into No. 13 the day before the Eastern party left, so as to be able to celebrate the occasion by having them all to an impromptu house-warming. There was not much to eat, and things were still a little unsettled; but Clover scrambled some eggs on her little blazer for them, the newly-lit fire burned cheerfully, and a good deal of quiet fun went on about it. Amy was so charmed with the minute establishment that she declared she meant to have one exactly like it for Mabel whenever she got married.

"And a spirit-lamp, too, just like Clover's, and a cunning, teeny-weeny kitchen and a stove to boil things on. Mamma, when shall I be old enough to have a house all of my own?"

"Not till you are tired of playing with dolls, I am afraid."

"Well, that will be never. If I thought I ever could be tired of Mabel, I should be so ashamed of myself that I should not know what to do. You oughtn't to say such things, Mamma; she might hear you, too, and have her feelings hurt. And please don't call her *that*," said Amy, who had as strong an objection to the word "doll" as mice are said to have to the word "cat."

Next morning the dear home people proceeded on their way, and Clover fell to work resolutely on her housekeeping, glad to keep busy, for she had a little fear of being homesick for Katy. Every small odd and end that she had brought with her from Burnet came into play now. The photographs were pinned on the wall, the few books and ornaments took their places on the extemporized shelves and on the table, which, thanks to Mrs. Hope, was no longer bare, but hidden by a big square of red canton flannel. There was almost always a little bunch of flowers from the Wade greenhouses, which were supposed to come from Mrs. Wade; and altogether the effect was cosey, and the little interior looked absolutely pretty, though the result was attained by such very simple means.

Phil thought it heavenly to be by themselves and out of the reach of strangers. Everything tasted delicious; all the arrangements pleased him; never was boy so easily suited as he for those first few weeks at No. 13.

"You're awfully good to me, Clover," he said one night rather suddenly, from the depths of his rocking-chair.

The remark was so little in Phil's line that it quite made her jump.

"Why, Phil, what made you say that?" she asked.

"Oh, I don't know. I was thinking about it. We used to call Katy the nicest, but you're just as good as she is. [This Clover justly considered a tremendous compliment.] You always make a fellow feel like home, as Geoff Templestowe says."

"Did Geoff say that?" with a warm sense of gladness at her heart. "How nice of him! What made him say it?"

"Oh, I don't know; it was up in the canyon one day when we got to talking," replied Phil. "There are no flies on you, he considers. I asked him once if he didn't think Miss Chase pretty, and he said not half so pretty as you were."

"Really! You seem to have been very confidential. And what is that about flies? Phil, Phil, you really mustn't use such slang."

"I suppose it is slang; but it's an awfully nice expression anyway."

"But what *does* it mean?"

"Oh, you must see just by the sound of it what it means,—that there's no nonsense sticking out all over you like some of the girls. It's a great compliment!"

"Is it? Well, I'm glad to know. But Mr. Templestowe never used such a phrase, I'm sure."

"No, he didn't," admitted Phil; "but that's what he meant."

So the winter drew on,—the strange, beautiful Colorado winter,—with weeks of golden sunshine broken by occasional storms of wind and sand, or by skurries of snow which made the plains white for a few hours and then vanished, leaving them dry and firm as before. The nights were often cold,—so cold that comfortables and blankets seemed all too few, and Clover roused with a shiver to think that presently it would be her duty to get up and start the fires so that Phil might find a warm house when he came downstairs. Then, before she knew it, fires would seem oppressive; first one window and then another would be thrown up, and Phil would be sitting on the piazza in the balmy sunshine as comfortable as on a June morning at home. It was a wonderful climate; and as Clover wrote her father, the winter was better even than the summer, and was certainly doing Phil more good. He was able to spend hours every day in the open air, walking, or riding Dr. Hope's horse, and improved steadily. Clover felt very happy about him.

This early rising and fire-making were the hardest things she had to encounter, though all the housekeeping proved more onerous than, in her inexperience, she had expected it to be. After the first week or two, however, she managed very well, and gradually learned the little labor-saving ways which can only be learned by actual experiment. Getting breakfast and tea she enjoyed, for they could be chiefly managed by the use of the chafing-dish. Dinners were more difficult, till she hit on the happy idea of having Mrs. Kenny roast a big piece of beef or mutton, or a pair of fowls every Monday. These *pièces de résistance* in their different stages of hot, cold, and warmed over, carried them well along through the week, and, supplemented with an occasional chop or steak, served very well. Fairly good soups could be bought in tins, which needed only to be seasoned and heated for use on table. Oysters were easily procurable there, as everywhere in the West; good brown-bread and rolls came from the bakery; and Clover developed a hitherto dormant talent for cookery and the making of Graham gems, corn-dodgers, hoe-cakes baked on a barrel head before the parlor fire, and wonderful little flaky biscuits raised all in a minute with Royal Baking Powder.

She also became expert in that other fine art of condensing work, and making it move in easy grooves. Her tea things she washed with her breakfast things, just setting the cups and plates in the sink for the night, pouring a dipper full of boiling water over them. There was no silver to care for, no delicate glass or valuable china; the very simplicity of apparatus made the house an easy one to keep. Clover was kept busy, for simplify as you will, providing for the daily needs of two persons does take time; but she liked her cares and rarely felt tired. The elastic and vigorous air seemed to build up her forces from moment to moment, and each day's fatigues were more than repaired by each night's rest, which is the balance of true health in living.

Little pleasures came from time to time. Christmas Day they spent with the Hopes, who from first to last proved the kindest and most helpful of friends to them. The young men from the High Valley were there also, and the day was brightly kept,—from the home letters by the early mail to the grand merry-making and dance with which it wound up. Everybody had some little present for everybody else. Mrs. Wade sent Clover a tall india-rubber plant in a china pot, which made a spire of green in the south window for the rest of the winter; and Clover had spent many odd moments and stitches in the fabrication of a gorgeous Mexican-worked sideboard cloth for the Hopes.

But of all Clover's offerings the one which pleased her most, as showing a close observation of her needs, came from Geoff Templestowe. It was a prosaic gift, being a wagon-load of piñon wood for the fire; but the gnarled, oddly twisted sticks were heaped high with pine boughs and long trails of red-fruited kinnikinnick to serve as a Christmas dressing, and somehow the gift gave Clover a peculiar pleasure.

"How dear of him!" she thought, lifting one of the big piñon logs with a gentle touch; "and how like him to think of it! I wonder what makes him so different from other people. He never says fine flourishing things like Thurber Wade, or abrupt, rather rude things like Clarence, or inconsiderate things like Phil, or satirical, funny things like the doctor; but he's always doing something kind. He's a little bit like papa, I think; and yet I don't know. I wish Katy could have seen him."

Life at St. Helen's in the winter season is never dull; but the gayest fortnight of all was when, late in January, the High Valley partners deserted their duties and came in for a visit to the Hopes. All sorts of small festivities had been saved for this special fortnight, and among the rest, Clover and Phil gave a party.

"If you can squeeze into the dining-room, and if you can do with just cream-toast for tea," she explained, "it would be such fun to have you come. I can't give you anything to eat to speak of, because I haven't any cook, you know; but you can all eat a great deal of dinner, and then you won't starve."

Thurber Wade, the Hopes, Clarence, Geoff, Marian, and Alice made a party of nine, and it was hard work indeed to squeeze so many into the tiny dining-room of No. 13. The very difficulties, however, made it all the jollier. Clover's cream-toast,—which she prepared before their eyes on the blazer,—her little tarts made of crackers split, buttered, and toasted brown with a spoonful of raspberry jam in each, and the big loaf of hot ginger-bread to be eaten with thick cream from the High Valley, were pronounced each in its way to be absolute perfection. Clarence and Phil kindly volunteered to "shunt the dishes" into the kitchen after the repast was concluded; and they gathered round the fire to play "twenty questions" and "stage-coach," and all manner of what Clover called "lead-pencil games,"—"crambo" and "criticism" and "anagrams" and "consequences." There was immense laughter over some of these, as, for instance, when Dr. Hope was reported as having met Mrs. Watson in the North Cheyenne Canyon, and he said that knowledge is power; and she, that when larks flew round ready roasted poor folks could stick a fork in; and the consequence was that they eloped together to a Cannibal Island where each suffered a process of disillusionation, and the world said it was the natural result of osculation. This last sentence was Phil's, and I fear he had peeped a little, or his context would not have been so apropos; but altogether the "cream-toast swarry," as he called it, was a pronounced success.

It was not long after this that a mysterious little cloud of difference seemed to fall on Thurber Wade. He ceased to call at No. 13, or to bring flowers from his mother; and by-and-by it was learned that he had started for a visit to the East. No one knew what had caused these phenomena, though some people may have suspected. Later it was announced that he was in Chicago and very attentive to a pretty Miss Somebody whose father had made a great deal of money in Standard oil. Poppy arched her brows and made great amused eyes at Clover, trying to entangle her into admissions as to this or that, and Clarence experimented in the same direction; but Clover was innocently impervious to these efforts, and no one ever knew what had happened between her and Thurber,—if, indeed, anything had happened.

So May came to St. Helen's in due course, of time. The sand-storms and the snow-storms were things of the past, the tawny yellow of the plains began to flush with green, and every day the sun grew more warm and beautiful. Phil seemed perfectly well and sound now; their occupancy of No. 13 was drawing to a close; and Clover, as she reflected that Colorado would soon be a thing of the past, and must be left behind, was sensible of a little sinking of the heart even though she and Phil were going home.

CHAPTER XI.

THE LAST OF THE CLOVER-LEAVES.

Last days are very apt to be hard days. As the time drew near for quitting No. 13, Clover was conscious of a growing reluctance.

"I wonder why it is that I mind it so much?" she asked herself. "Phil has got well here, to be sure; that would be enough of itself to make me fond of the place, and we have had a happy winter in this little house. But still, papa, Elsie, John,—it seems very queer that I am not gladder to go back to them. I can't account for it. It isn't natural, and it seems wrong in me."

It was a rainy afternoon in which Clover made these reflections. Phil, weary of being shut indoors, had donned ulster and overshoes, and gone up to make a call on Mrs. Hope. Clover was quite alone in the house, as she sat with her mending-basket beside the fireplace, in which was burning the last but three of the piñon logs,—Geoff Templestowe's Christmas present.

"They will just last us out," reflected Clover; "what a comfort they have been! I would like to carry the very last of them home with me, and keep it to look at; but I suppose it would be silly."

She looked about the little room. Nothing as yet had been moved or disturbed, though the next week would bring their term of occupancy to a close.

"This is a good evening to begin to take things down and pack them," she thought. "No one is likely to come in, and Phil is away."

She rose from her chair, moved restlessly to and fro, and at last leaned forward and unpinned a corner of one of the photographs on the wall. She stood for a moment irresolutely with the pin in her fingers, then she jammed it determinedly back into the photograph again, and returned to her sewing. I almost think there were tears in her eyes.

"No," she said half aloud, "I won't spoil it yet. We'll have one more pleasant night with everything just as it is, and then I'll go to work and pull all to pieces at once. It's the easiest way."

Just then a foot sounded on the steps, and a knock was heard. Clover opened the door, and gave an exclamation of pleasure. It was Geoffrey Templestowe, splashed and wet from a muddy ride down the pass, but wearing a very bright face.

"How nice and unexpected this is!" was Clover's greeting. "It is such a bad day that I didn't suppose you or Clarence could possibly get in. Come to the fire and warm yourself. Is he here too?"

"No; he is out at the ranch. I came in to meet a man on business; but it seems there's a wash-out somewhere between here and Santa Fé, and my man telegraphs that he can't get through till to-morrow noon."

"So you will spend the night in town."

"Yes. I took Marigold to the stable, and spoke to Mrs. Marsh about a room, and then I walked up to see you and Phil. How is he, by the way?"

"Quite well. I never saw him so strong or so jolly. Papa will hardly believe his eyes when we get back. He has gone up to the Hopes, but will be in presently. You'll stay and take tea with us, of course."

"Thanks, if you will have me; I was hoping to be asked."

"Oh, we're only too glad to have you. Our time here is getting so short that we want to make the very most of all our friends; and by good luck there is a can of oysters in the house, so I can give you something hot."

"Do you really go so soon?"

"Our lease is out next week, you know."

"Really; so soon as that?"

"It isn't soon. We have lived here nearly eight months."

"What a good time we have all had in this little house!" cried Geoff, regretfully. "It has been a sort of warm little centre to us homeless people all winter."

"You don't count yourself among the homeless ones, I hope, with such a pleasant place as the High Valley to live in."

"Oh, the hut is all very well in its way, of course; but I don't look at it as a home exactly. It answers to eat and sleep in, and for a shelter when it rains; but you can't make much more of it than that. The only time it ever seemed home-like in the least was when you and Mrs. Hope were there. That week spoiled it for me for all time."

"That's a pity, if it's true, but I hope it isn't. It was a delightful week, though; and I think you do the valley an injustice. It's a beautiful place. Now, if you will excuse me, I am going to get supper."

"Let me help you."

"Oh, there is almost nothing to do. I'd much rather you would sit still and rest. You are tired from your ride, I'm sure; and if you don't mind, I'll bring my blazer and cook the oysters here by the fire. I always did like to 'kitch in the dining-room,' as Mrs. Whitney calls it."

Clover had set the tea-table before she sat down to sew, so there really was almost nothing to do. Geoff lay back in his chair and looked on with a sort of dreamy pleasure as she went lightly to and fro, making her arrangements, which, simple as they were, had a certain dainty quality about them which seemed peculiar to all that Clover did,—twisted a trail of kinnikinnick about the butter-plate, laid a garnish of fresh parsley on the slices of cold beef, and set a glass full of wild crocuses in the middle of the table. Then she returned to the parlor, put the kettle, which had already begun to sing, on the fire, and began to stir and season her oysters, which presently sent out a savory smell.

"I have learned six ways of cooking oysters this winter," she announced gleefully. "This is a dry-pan-roast. I wonder if you'll approve of it. And I wonder why Phil doesn't come. I wish he would make haste, for these are nearly done."

"There he is now," remarked Geoff.

But instead it was Dr. Hope's office-boy with a note.

DEAR C.,—Mrs. Hope wants me for a fourth hand at whist, so I'm

staying, if you don't mind. She says if it didn't pour so she'd
ask you to come too. P.

"Well, I'm glad," said Clover. "It's been a dull day for him, and now he'll
have a pleasant evening, only he'll miss you."

"I call it very inconsiderate of the little scamp," observed Geoff. "He doesn't
know but that he's leaving you to spend the evening quite alone."

"Oh, boys don't think of things like that."

"Boys ought to, then. However, I can stand his absence, if you can!"

It was a very merry little meal to which they presently sat down, full of the
charm which the unexpected brings with it. Clover had grown to regard Geoff
as one of her very best friends, and was perfectly at her ease with him, while to
him, poor lonely fellow, such a glimpse of cosey home-life was like a peep at
Paradise. He prolonged the pleasure as much as possible, ate each oyster slowly,
descanting on its flavor, and drank more cups of tea than were at all good for
him, for the pleasure of having Clover pour them out. He made no further
offers of help when supper was ended, but looked on with fascinated eyes as she
cleared away and made things tidy.

At last she finished and came back to the fire. There was a silence. Geoff
was first to break it. "It would seem like a prison to you, I am afraid," he said
abruptly.

"What would?"

"I was thinking of what you said about the High Valley."

"Oh!"

"You've only seen it in summer, you know. It's quite a different place in the
winter. I don't believe a—person—could live on the year round and be
contented."

"It would depend upon the person, of course."

"If it were a lady,—yourself, for instance,—could it be made anyway
tolerable, do you think? Of course, one might get away now and then—"

"I don't know. It's not easy to tell beforehand how people are going to feel;
but I can't imagine the High Valley ever seeming like a prison," replied Clover,
vexed to find herself blushing, and yet unable to help it, Geoff's manner had
such an odd intensity in it.

"If I were sure that you could realize what it would be—" he began
impetuously; then quieting himself, "but you don't. How could you? Ranch life is
well enough in summer for a short time by way of a frolic; but in winter and
spring with the Upper Canyon full of snow, and the road down muddy and
slippery, and the storms and short days, and the sense of being shut in and
lonely, it would be a dismal place for a lady. Nobody has a right to expect a
woman to undergo such a life."

Clover absorbed herself in her sewing, she did not speak; but still that deep
uncomfortable blush burned on her cheeks.

"What do you think?" persisted Geoff. "Wouldn't it be inexcusable
selfishness in a man to ask such a thing?"

"I think;" said Clover, shyly and softly, "that a man has a right to ask for whatever he wants, and—" she paused.

"And—what?" urged Geoff, bending forward.

"Well, a woman has always the right to say no, if she doesn't want to say yes."

"You tempt me awfully," cried Geoff, starting up. "When I think what this place is going to seem like after you've gone, and what the ranch will be with all the heart taken from it, and the loneliness made twice as lonely by comparison, I grow desperate, and feel as if I could not let you go without at least risking the question. But Clover,—let me call you so this once,—no woman could consent to such a life unless she cared very much for a man. Could you ever love me well enough for that, do you think?"

"It seems to me a very unfair sort of question to put," said Clover, with a mischievous glint in her usually soft eyes. "Suppose I said I could, and then you turned round and remarked that you were ever so sorry that you couldn't reciprocate my feelings—"

"Clover," catching her hand, "how can you torment me so? Is it necessary that I should tell you that I love you with every bit of heart that is in me, and need you and want you and long for you, but have never dared to hope that you could want me? Loveliest, sweetest, I do, and I always shall, whether it is yes or no."

"Then, Geoff—if you feel like that—if you're quite sure you feel like that, I think—"

"What do you think, dearest?"

"I think—that I could be very happy even in winter—in the High Valley."

And papa and the children, and the lonely and far-away feelings? There was never a mention of them in this frank acceptance. Oh, Clover, Clover, circumstances *do* alter cases!

Mrs. Hope's rubber of whist seemed a long one, for Phil did not get home till a quarter before eleven, by which time the two by the fire had settled the whole progress of their future lives, while the last logs of the piñon wood crackled, smouldered, and at length broke apart into flaming brands. In imagination the little ranch house had thrown out as many wings and as easily as a newly-hatched dragon-fly, had been beautified and made convenient in all sorts of ways,—a flower-garden had sprouted round its base, plenty of room had been made for papa and the children and Katy and Ned, who were to come out continually for visits in the long lovely summers; they themselves also were to go to and fro,—to Burnet, and still farther afield, over seas to the old Devonshire grange which Geoff remembered so fondly.

"How my mother and Isabel will delight in you," he said; "and the squire! You are precisely the girl to take his fancy. We'll go over and see them as soon as we can, won't we, Clover?"

Clover listened delightedly to all these schemes, but through them all, like that young Irish lady who went over the marriage service with her lover adding at the end of every clause, "Provided my father gives his consent," she interposed a little running thread of protest,—"If papa is willing. You know, Geoff, I can't really promise anything till I've talked with papa."

It was settled that until Dr. Carr had been consulted, the affair was not to be called an engagement, or spoken of to any one; only Clover asked Geoff to tell Clarence all about it at once.

The thought of Clarence was, in truth, the one cloud in her happiness just then. It was impossible to calculate how he would take the news. If it made him angry or very unhappy, if it broke up his friendship with Geoff, and perhaps interfered with their partnership so that one or other of them must leave the High Valley, Clover felt that it would grievously mar her contentment. There was no use in planning anything till they knew how he would feel and act. In any case, she realized that they were bound to consider him before themselves, and make it as easy and as little painful as possible. If he were vexatious, they must be patient; if sulky, they must be forbearing.

Phil opened his eyes very wide at the pair sitting so coseyly over the fire when at last he came in.

"I say, have *you* been here all the evening?" he cried. "Well, that's a sell! I wouldn't have gone out if I'd known."

"We've missed you very much," quoth Geoff; and then he laughed as at some extremely good joke, and Clover laughed too.

"You seem to have kept up your spirits pretty well, considering," remarked Phil, dryly. Boys of eighteen are not apt to enjoy jokes which do not originate with themselves; they are suspicious of them.

"I suppose I must go now," said Geoff, looking at his watch; "but I shall see you again before I leave. I'll come in to-morrow after I've met my man."

"All right," said Phil; "I won't go out till you come."

"Oh, pray don't feel obliged to stay in. I can't at all tell when I shall be able to get through with the fellow."

"Come to dinner if you can," suggested Clover. "Phil is sure to be at home then."

Lovers are like ostriches. Geoff went away just shaking hands casually, and was very particular to say "Miss Carr;" and he and Clover felt that they had managed so skilfully and concealed their secret so well; yet the first remark made by Phil as the door shut was, "Geoff seems queer to-night, somehow, and so do you. What have you been talking about all the evening?"

An observant younger brother is a difficult factor in a love affair.

Two days passed. Clover looked in vain for a note from the High Valley to say how Clarence had borne the revelation; and she grew more nervous with every hour. It was absolutely necessary now to dismantle the house, and she found a certain relief in keeping exceedingly busy. Somehow the break-up had lost its inexplicable pain, and a glad little voice sang all the time at her heart, "I shall come back; I shall certainly come back. Papa will let me, I am sure, when he knows Geoff, and how nice he is."

She was at the dining-table wrapping a row of books in paper ready for packing, when a step sounded, and glancing round she saw Clarence himself standing in the doorway. He did not look angry, as she had feared he might, or moody; and though he avoided her eye at first, his face was resolute and kind.

"Geoff has told me," were his first words. "I know from what he said that you, and he too, are afraid that I shall make myself disagreeable; so I've come in to say that I shall do nothing of the kind."

"Dear Clarence, that wasn't what Geoff meant, or I either," said Clover, with a rush of relief, and holding out both her hands to him; "what we were afraid of was that you might be unhappy."

"Well," in a husky tone, and holding the little hands very tight, "it isn't easy, of course, to give up a hope. I've held on to mine all this time, though I've told myself a hundred times that I was a fool for doing so, and though I knew in my heart it was no use. Now I've had two days to think it over and get past the first shock, and, Clover, I've decided. You and Geoff are the best friends I've got in the world. I never seemed to make friends, somehow. Till you came to Hillsover that time nobody liked me much; I don't know why. I can't get along without you two; so I give you up without any hard feeling, and I mean to be as jolly as I can about it. After all, to have you at the High Valley will be a sort of happiness, even if you don't come for my sake exactly," with an attempt at a laugh.

"Clarence, you really are a dear boy! I can't tell you how I thank you, and how I admire you for being so nice about this."

"Then that's worth something, too. I'd do a good deal to win your approval, Clover. So it's all settled. Don't worry about me, or be afraid that I shall spoil your comfort with sour looks. If I find I can't stand it, I'll go away for a while; but I don't think it'll come to that. You'll make a real home out of the ranch house, and you'll let me have my share of your life, and be a brother to you and Geoff; and I'll try to be a good one."

Clover was touched to the heart by these manful words so gently spoken.

"You shall be our dear special brother always," she said. "Only this was needed to make me quite happy. I am so glad you don't want to go away and leave us, or to have us leave you. We'll make the ranch over into the dearest little home in the world, and be so cosey there all together, and papa and the others shall come out for visits; and you'll like them so much, I know, Elsie especially."

"Does she look like you?"

"Not a bit; she's ever so much prettier."

"I don't believe a word of that"

Clover's heart being thus lightened of its only burden by this treaty of mutual amity, she proceeded joyously with her packing. Mrs. Hope said she was not half sorry enough to go away, and Poppy upbraided her as a gay deceiver without any conscience or affections. She laughed and protested and denied, but looked so radiantly satisfied the while as to give a fair color for her friends' accusations, especially as she could not explain the reasons of her contentment or hint at her hopes of return. Mrs. Hope probably had her suspicions, for she was rather urgent with Clover to leave this thing and that for safe keeping "in case you ever come back;" but Clover declined these offers, and resolutely packed up everything with a foolish little superstition that it was "better luck" to do so, and that papa would like it better.

Quite a little group of friends assembled at the railway station to see her and Phil set off. They were laden with flowers and fruit and "natural soda-water" with which to beguile the long journey, and with many good wishes and affectionate hopes that they might return some day.

"Something tells me that you will," Mrs. Hope declared. "I feel it in my bones, and they hardly ever deceive me. My mother had the same kind; it's in the family."

"Something tells me that you must," cried Poppy, embracing Clover; "but I'm afraid it isn't bones or anything prophetic, but only the fact that I want you to so very much."

From the midst of these farewells Clover's eyes crossed the valley and sought out Mount Cheyenne.

"How differently I should be feeling," she thought, "if this were going away with no real hope of coming back! I could hardly have borne to look at you had that been the case, you dear beautiful thing; but I *am* coming back to live close beside you always, and oh, how glad I am!"

"Is that good-by to Cheyenne?" asked Marian, catching the little wave of a hand.

"Yes, it *is* good-by; but I have promised him that it shall soon be how-do-you-do again. Mount Cheyenne and I understand each other."

"I know; you have always had a sentimental attachment to that mountain. Now Pike's Peak is *my* affinity. We get on beautifully together."

"Pike's Peak indeed! I am ashamed of you."

Then the train moved away amid a flutter of handkerchiefs, but still Clover and Phil were not left to themselves; for Dr. Hope, who had a consultation in Denver, was to see them safely off in the night express, and Geoff had some real or invented business which made it necessary for him to go also.

Clover carried with her through all the three days' ride the lingering pressure of Geoff's hand, and his whispered promise to "come on soon." It made the long way seem short. But when they arrived, amid all the kisses and rejoicings, the exclamations over Phil's look of health and vigor, the girls' intense interest in all that she had seen and done, papa's warm approval of her management, her secret began to burn guiltily within her. What *would* they all say when they knew?

And what did they say? I think few of you will be at a loss to guess. Life— real life as well as life in story-books—is full of such shocks and surprises. They are half happy, half unhappy; but they have to be borne. Younger sisters, till their own turns come, are apt to take a severe view of marriage plans, and to feel that they cruelly interrupt a past order of things which, so far as they are concerned, need no improvement. And parents, who say less and understand better, suffer, perhaps, more. "To bear, to rear, to lose," is the order of family history, generally unexpected, always recurring.

But true love is not selfish. In time it accustoms itself to anything which secures happiness for its object. Dr. Carr did confide to Katy in a moment of private explosion that he wished the Great West had never been invented, and that such a prohibitory tax could be laid upon young Englishmen as to make it impossible that another one should ever be landed on our shores; but he had never in his life refused Clover anything upon which she had set her heart, and he saw in her eyes that her heart was very much set on this. John and Elsie scolded and cried, and then in time began to talk of their future visits to High Valley till they grew to anticipate them, and be rather in a hurry for them to begin. Geoff's arrival completed their conversion.

"Nicer than Ned," Johnnie pronounced him; and even Dr. Carr was forced to confess that the sons-in-law with which Fate had provided him were of a superior sort; only he wished that they didn't want to marry *his* girls!

Phil, from first to last, was in favor of the plan, and a firm ally to the lovers. He had grown extremely Western in his ideas, and was persuaded in his mind that "this old East," as he termed it, with its puny possibilities, did not amount to much, and that as soon as he was old enough to shape his own destinies, he should return to the only section of the country worthy the attention of a young man of parts. Meanwhile, he was perfectly well again, and willing to comply with his father's desire that before he made any positive arrangements for his future, he should get a sound and thorough education.

"So you are actually going out to the wild and barbarous West, to live on a ranch, milk cows, chase the wild buffalo to its lair, and hold the tiger-cat by its favorite forelock," wrote Rose Red. "What was that you were saying only the other day about nice convenient husbands, who cruise off for 'good long times,' and leave their wives comfortably at home with their own families? And here you are planning to marry a man who, whenever he isn't galloping after cattle, will be in your pocket at home! Oh, Clover, Clover, how inconsistent a thing is woman,—not to say girl,—and what havoc that queer deity named Cupid does make with preconceived opinions! I did think I could rely on you; but you are just as bad as the rest of us, and when a lad whistles, go off after him wherever he happens to lead, and think it the best thing possible to do so. It's a mad world, my masters; and I'm thankful that Roslein is only four and a half years old."

And Clover's answer was one line on a postal card,—
"Guilty, but recommended to mercy!"

Echo Library

www.echo-library.com

Echo Library uses advanced digital print-on-demand technology to build and preserve an exciting world class collection of rare and out-of-print books, making them readily available for everyone to enjoy.

Situated just yards from Teddington Lock on the River Thames, Echo Library was founded in 2005 by Tom Cherrington, a specialist dealer in rare and antiquarian books with a passion for literature.

Please visit our website for a complete catalogue of our books, which includes foreign language titles.

The Right to Read

Echo Library actively supports the Royal National Institute of the Blind's Right to Read initiative by publishing a comprehensive range of large print and clear print titles.

Large Print titles are in 16 point Tiresias font as recommended by the RNIB.

Clear Print titles are in 13 point Tiresias font and designed for those who find standard print difficult to read.

Customer Service

If there is a serious error in the text or layout please send details to feedback@echo-library.com and we will supply a corrected copy. If there is a printing fault or the book is damaged please refer to your supplier.

Lightning Source UK Ltd.
Milton Keynes UK
07 November 2009

145921UK00002B/222/A

9 781406 848502